What
abc

MW01615721

"R.J. Patterson does a fantastic job at keeping you engaged and interested. I look forward to more from this talented author."

- Aaron Patterson
bestselling author of SWEET DREAMS

DEAD SHOT

"Small town life in southern Idaho might seem quaint and idyllic to some. But when local newspaper reporter Cal Murphy begins to uncover a series of strange deaths that are linked to a sticky spider web of deception, the lid on the peaceful town is blown wide open. Told with all the energy and bravado of an old pro, first-timer R.J. Patterson hits one out of the park his first time at bat with *Dead Shot*. It's that good."

- Vincent Zandri
bestselling author of THE REMAINS

"You can tell R.J. knows what it's like to live in the newspaper world, but with *Dead Shot*, he's proven that he also can write one heck of a murder mystery."

- Josh Katzowitz
NFL writer for CBSSports.com
& author of Sid Gillman: Father of the Passing Game

"Patterson has a mean streak about a mile wide and puts his two main characters through quite a horrible ride, which makes for good reading."

- Richard D., reader

DEAD LINE

"This book kept me on the edge of my seat the whole time. I didn't really want to put it down. R.J. Patterson has hooked me. I'll be back for more."

- Bob Behler
3-time Idaho broadcaster of the year
and play-by-play voice for Boise State football

"Like a John Grisham novel, from the very start I was pulled right into the story and couldn't put the book down. It was as if I personally knew and cared about what happened to each of the main characters. Every chapter ended with so much excitement and suspense I had to continue to read until I learned how it ended, even though it kept me up until 3:00 A.M.

*- **Ray F.**, reader*

DEAD IN THE WATER

"In Dead in the Water, R.J. Patterson accurately captures the action-packed saga of a what could be a real-life college football scandal. The sordid details will leave readers flipping through the pages as fast as a hurry-up offense."

- Mark Schlabach,
ESPN college sports columnist and
co-author of *Called to Coach*
and *Heisman: The Man Behind the Trophy*

THE WARREN OMISSIONS

"What can be more fascinating than a super high concept novel that reopens the conspiracy behind the JFK assassination while the threat of a global world war rests in the balance? With his new novel, *The Warren Omissions*, former journalist turned bestselling author R.J. Patterson proves he just might be the next worthy successor to Vince Flynn."

*- **Vincent Zandri***
bestselling author of THE REMAINS

OTHER TITLES BY
R.J. PATTERSON

Cal Murphy Thrillers
Dead Shot
Dead Line
Better off Dead
Dead in the Water
Dead Man's Curve
Dead and Gone
Dead Wrong
Dead Man's Land
Dead Drop
Dead to Rights
Dead End

James Flynn Thrillers
The Warren Omissions
Imminent Threat
The Cooper Affair
Seeds of War

Brady Hawk Thrillers
First Strike
Deep Cover
Point of Impact
Full Blast
Target Zero
Fury
State of Play
Siege
Seek and Destroy
Into the Shadows
Hard Target
No Way Out

FULL BLAST

A Brady Hawk novel

R.J. PATTERSON

For Brian, a good friend with integrity and compassion

CHAPTER 0

Prague, Czech Republic
Pachtuv Palace Hotel

BRADY HAWK WISHED HE WAS sitting on a sunny beach somewhere drinking his favorite Kentucky bourbon. Instead, he lay in a prone position between two hotel beds, his gun trained on a would-be assassin bound to a plush office chair directly in front of him. Hunkered down in the room, Hawk contemplated his next course of action. He needed answers from the man seated a few feet away, answers the man wasn't ready to give up. But Hawk's options were limited.

In the hallway, he heard the security personnel following lockdown protocol, knocking on one door at a time as they neared their room. Yet, Hawk wasn't convinced they were with the hotel. Based on the speed at which the men were clearing rooms, he guessed they were only two doors away.

"You need to start talking now," Hawk said, his gaze darting back and forth between the man and the door.

The man sighed and shook his head before glaring defiantly. "What difference does it make?" he asked. "I'm dead if I talk; I'm dead if I don't. So, I'd rather die with some of my principles still intact."

"If you were sent here to assassinate Jordanian Prime Minister Yaseen Abbadi, you have no principles."

"Sweet irony getting a lecture from you about principles," the man said. "The man who routinely defies orders and puts others at risk in doing so."

Hawk narrowed his eyes. "You think you know who I am?"

"Everybody knows about the great Brady Hawk . . . and his treasonous acts against the United States government."

"Treasonous?" Hawk huffed. "That's a good one. Be sure to give your script writer a raise."

"You think I'm joking?"

Hawk shook his head, eyeing the man closely. "Think *I'm* joking?"

Hawk tightened the silencer on his gun and took aim at the man's foot. The man let out a loud moan as a bullet ripped through his shoe. Fragments of leather and blood splatters dotted the floor around him.

"They're gonna hear us, you know," the man said.

Hawk shrugged. "I'm more interested in hearing what you have to say about your mission. Who are you working for? Searchlight? The Chamber? Who? My patience is running thin."

The man broke into laughter. "You really don't have a clue, do you? Sure is surprising given how they act like you're the gold standard among assassins."

"What are you talking about?"

The men's voices grew louder yet again. Hawk figured they were only one room away now.

"Getting a little nervous?" the man asked. "Well, you should be. Your little escapade here is about to come to a screeching halt, one way or another."

"If I had a nickel for every time someone told me that, I'd be doing what I'd rather be doing about now—sitting on a beach in a Pacific isle, reading a good book, and drinking bourbon. But instead, I'm stuck in here with a detestable puke who refuses to tell me what I need to know."

"I'm more or less stalling because I want to see how you intend to get out of this thing."

"Don't think you'll be around to see it."

In the hallway, doors slammed and heavy foot-falls echoed near their room. The handle barely moved before a string of shots down the hallway arrested their attention. It was followed by the sound of at least three men dashing off in the direction of the gunfire.

Hawk let out a small sigh, pleased that he could focus all his attention on the incompliant prisoner.

"They'll be back," the man said, grimacing.

"Start talking," Hawk said as he remained prone. "I can wait you out, you know."

Hawk fired another round into the man's left foot, producing the same results. "My next shot will be your knee."

The man howled in pain, twisting and turning in his seat. For a moment, Hawk thought the man might be trying wriggle free, but Hawk knew there was no way he'd break out.

"Okay, okay," the man said. "I'll tell you what you wanna know."

Before he could utter another word, a bullet ripped through the window, shattering it. Then two more rounds promptly followed.

Hawk watched the man go limp and then lifeless. Two shots to the chest, one to the head. It was over before Hawk could get a single answer.

Crawling on his stomach, he moved forward a few feet and reached the man's gun he'd kicked aside during their initial confrontation. As he stared at the familiar weapon, he immediately knew the man's employer: CIA.

Hawk took a deep breath and exhaled slowly.

Based on the man's comments, apparently Hawk had been deemed a traitor by the U.S. government. Fighting terrorists was one thing, but his own government? Hawk shuddered at where his journey had led him. He never wanted *this*. But he'd ventured into territory that made no allowances for backtracking. This was his path, a new one he would have to navigate cautiously. And his first step began with surviving the sniper perched somewhere outside his room.

Hawk needed to get out of there as soon as possible. Someone had been watching and listening to their entire exchange before killing the CIA agent. And Hawk didn't doubt for a second that he was next.

CHAPTER 1

Five days earlier
San Francisco, California
AT&T Park

HAWK GLANCED AT HIS TICKET STUB as the attendant handed it back to him. The last time he'd watched a game at AT&T Park was during a trip to see his grandmother during his senior year of high school. Before his time with the Navy Seals, he'd never been much of a baseball fan, attending games only at the request of his family. But during his training in San Diego, the baseball bug bit him hard and Hawk adopted not only the Padres as his team but baseball as his sport.

After begrudgingly going to games years ago, Hawk couldn't wait to grab his seat and watch an exciting matchup between two of the sport's best pitchers in Madison Bumgarner and Clayton Kershaw. He settled into his seat on the next-to-last row in the upper deck facing the first base foul line. With a deep breath, he inhaled the smell of grilled food wafting along the light bay breeze. He closed his eyes for a few seconds as well to take in the sounds of the stadium—the vendor calling out "ice cold beeeeer," the pop of the baseball against a catcher's mitt, and the background track of ambient organ music over the loudspeaker. With such a perfect late spring evening, Hawk wondered why he hadn't attended a game on his own volition much sooner.

But he wasn't even at this game at his own choosing. J.B. Blunt, his boss at Firestorm, had made it clear in no uncertain terms that attendance wasn't optional. Not that Hawk minded.

He bought a beer and a bag of peanuts, which he worked his way through slowly. Bumgarner and Kershaw, however, moved quickly through their opponents' lineups in what was shaping up to be an exciting finish. By the middle of the seventh inning, Hawk had almost forgotten he was there to meet with Blunt, a fact he recalled only when he felt a firm tap on his shoulder.

"Don't turn around," Blunt said.

Hawk obeyed and kept his eyes on the field. He leaned back to make sure Blunt could hear him when he spoke.

"I didn't think you were going to make it," Hawk

said. "Not that I minded. This has been one heckuva ball game."

"I've got a new assignment for you."

"And I've got some questions for you."

Blunt sighed. "I'm not sure I can answer them."

"Will you at least try?"

"I'll give it a shot. Go ahead."

Hawk rubbed the back of his head with his hand, remaining pensive before speaking. "What are we doing here?" A pause. "I mean, what is the end game of Firestorm?"

"I'm still trying to figure that out myself."

"You mean you don't have a plan?"

Blunt chuckled. "No, no. That's not what I mean at all. We have a plan, but it's changed severely in the past few weeks. People I thought were my friends I've learned are now my enemies. The world's not as black and white as it used to be."

"The world's never been black or white, just various shades of gray."

"Which brings me to my next assignment for you."

Hawk shifted in his seat and kept his eyes trained on the field. "I'm not sure I can comply if I don't know where we're headed."

"We're all headed for disaster if we don't stop one of our biggest allies in the fight against terrorism from getting assassinated."

"I've heard this song before, one that's followed up with another leader singing the same tune, until he decides to rebel."

Blunt laughed before his chuckling devolved into a cough. "Your cynicism in this job suits you well, Hawk. But grave danger awaits us all if we allow the best men in this world to die at the hands of those who have a vested interest in perpetrating war."

"So, what's the assignment?"

"Yaseen Abbadi, the Jordanian prime minister, requires protection at a summit in Prague this week at the Pachtuv Palace Hotel. He's scheduled to speak late Thursday afternoon at which time I hear there will be an attempt on his life."

"And what's his sin?" Hawk asked.

"Trying to bring together different interests in the Middle East for the sake of peace and stability. Abbadi has been working to convince several leaders that a new partnership would benefit all nations involved, not to mention give them a bigger voice on the international stage."

"Why not take out or threaten the potential partners?"

"Nothing makes a statement quite like a public assassination."

Hawk drank a big swig of his beer. "Who wants him out of the way?"

"*Who doesn't* is the better question."

Hawk watched Kershaw strike out Buster Posey for the final out of the seventh inning before resuming their covert conversation. "Al Hasib? Searchlight? The Chamber?"

"Try all of the above."

Hawk shook his head.

"I'm not sure I'll be able to do this on my own. Alex isn't exactly on board with Firestorm at the moment. Searchlight's attempts to woo her have been incredibly strong, not to mention one of their agents, Kade Parker, saved her life."

"If anybody can convince her to reaffirm her commitment to Firestorm, it's you, Hawk. Just invite her over for a Bollywood marathon. She'll be like putty in your hands."

Hawk smiled. "You make it sound so simple."

"That's what my ex-wife used to tell me."

Blunt stood up and stepped into the aisle, walking down to the same row as Hawk before stopping. "So, can I count on you, Hawk?"

Hawk nodded. "Where are you gonna be?"

"Hopefully, where no one can find me.'"

CHAPTER 2

Monday
National Archives
Washington, D.C.

HAWK CHECKED HIS WATCH and hustled up the steps of the National Archive Building in downtown Washington. Aside from his aversion to being late, he always liked to get an idea of all entry and exit points in a building just in case something happened. It could be a debilitating practice, yet he refused to resist the urge whenever he entered an unfamiliar location.

With the desire to watch his steps, Hawk decided to change up his usual meeting venue with Alex. Their normal spot at the National Archive building in College Park was too open. They needed a place with more privacy, and the downtown building provided just that.

Hawk flashed his archives ID badge and made his way to the second floor. He passed the time waiting for Alex's arrival by scrolling through the news on his phone. An article about political gridlock. More racial unrest after police shot an unarmed man. Hollywood power couple getting divorced.

It's as if we're on some cosmic hamster wheel.

Then there was an article that caught Hawk's eye. *G-8 Leaders to Meet in Washington* blared the headline. Hawk read about how diplomats from Canada, France, Germany, Italy, Japan, Russia, the United Kingdom, and the United States were scheduled to gather in the nation's capital to discuss new cooperative security measures to make it more difficult for terrorist groups to move between countries as well as transfer funds.

Senator Mark Adams, head of the U.S. Senate Committee on Homeland Security and Governmental Affairs, was excited about the potential outcomes of the gathering, according to the article. "I believe that this type of cooperative endeavor will only strengthen the safety of the free world and make life more difficult on those who seek to destroy the freedoms we've all worked so diligently to have," Adams was quoted as saying.

Hawk laughed softly to himself as he read the words. Germany, Italy, Japan, Russia, and even the United Kingdom all stood as enemies of the United States at one time or another. Yet, here they were, banding together for the good of the free world. And while Adams's talking points sounded great in theory, Hawk wasn't sure any one country or group needed to possess such power. He believed that kind of power always seemed to lead to some type of unnecessary conflict.

"What's so funny?" Alex asked as she walked up to Hawk.

He didn't even realize a wry grin still remained on his face.

"Oh, nothing, really," he said, putting his phone into his pocket. "I'm glad you could make it."

Alex sat down. "I figured I owed it to you to hear you out one more time, even if I know what you're going to say."

Hawk interlocked his fingers and then placed his hands on the table in front of him. "So, what you're saying is that I'll be wasting my time."

She nodded. "Pretty much."

Hawk's shoulders slumped. "I don't know what I need to say to convince you to change your mind, but I need the words right now because I need you with me. We're a team, Alex."

"*Were* a team," she corrected, wagging her right index finger at him.

"What makes Searchlight that much more of an attractive option for you? You know nothing about them."

"I know more than you might think, and quite frankly I don't have enough time to enumerate all the issues I have with Firestorm and Blunt."

"But what do you really know about Search-light?"

"I know that Kade Parker saved my life, and he gave me plenty to think about concerning Blunt."

Hawk shook his head slowly and gazed at the ceiling. After a long sigh, he turned his attention back toward Alex. "How do you know that attack wasn't all staged?"

Alex smiled and patted Hawk's hands. "You're really perfect for this job, you know?"

Hawk crossed his arms and leaned back in his chair.

"This isn't like you. I-I just don't understand why you'd want to join an organization that wants me dead."

"I can protect you."

"But will you?"

"Hawk, what's this really about? Do you have feelings for me? If you do, just say so."

Hawk eyed her closely. "Would it make a difference if I did?"

"At this point? *No.*" Alex stood up and walked around the table before patting him on the back. "Good luck, Hawk. I'm sure you're doing what's best for you. I've got to do what's best for me."

She took a few steps before Hawk spoke again.

"Would a Bollywood marathon change your mind?" he asked.

Alex stopped and turned around. "Did Blunt tell you to say that?"

He nodded. "It was worth a shot."

"Goodbye, Hawk."

He watched as she walked away. If he was honest with himself, he definitely had feelings for her. But they weren't easy feelings to sort out. They'd been to battle together. Their teamwork saved lives, hundreds, if not thousands, of lives. And she seemed eager to throw it away. But for what? A more transparent boss? A clearer mission?

Hawk couldn't deny Blunt's Firestorm operation contained flaws, chief among them was the leader himself. But it wasn't a strong enough reason to walk away. Hawk had been afforded to do the kind of work he wanted to do after he understood the seriousness of the threat terrorists imposed on every person who lived on planet Earth. He'd experienced the loss they could inflict on a person. And all for what? To gain a little more power on their part of the rock? To lash out at some ideals they didn't understand or detested as prescribed by their religion? It was all too much for him to stand by idly. Yet Hawk understood this kind of undertaking required a cooperative effort. No matter how well he operated as a solo operative, he was never truly on his own—at least, he didn't want to be.

He waited until she disappeared into the stairwell before he counted to a hundred beneath his breath. It was a simple protocol they'd established to make sure they weren't in an open place at the same time. According to Blunt, they weren't even supposed to meet, publicly or privately, but they stopped adhering to that rule after his mission in Zaranj. However, this procedure still made sense to Hawk.

He trudged toward the stairwell and exited the building. Stopping at the bottom of the National Archive building steps, he scanned the sidewalk running parallel to Constitution Avenue for her. After a few seconds, he spotted her on the sidewalk near the southwest corner of the block. Almost immediately, three men surrounded her and pushed her toward a van facing north parked along the side of 9th Street.

Hawk watched for a few seconds, unsure if he needed to help her or not. By the time he realized she was resisting, it was too late. He sprinted along the sidewalk toward her, but by the time he reached the corner, the van door had slammed shut before the vehicle lurched forward down the road.

All Hawk could do was watch. He'd never felt so helpless since before joining Firestorm—or alone.

CHAPTER 3

International Waters
30 miles offshore from California

BLUNT SPLASHED THE SIDE OF HIS GLASS with scotch as his boat, the *Pequod*, rocked with the waves. He uttered a few expletives under his breath before he picked up his glass to steady it. Waiting for a moment of peace on the open waters so he could pour cleanly, he gazed at the horizon. Other than an occasional fish leaping out of the water, Blunt struggled to find any more signs of life. It was how he liked it—at least under the given circumstances.

He took a long pull on his scotch before resting the glass on the table. The serenity he experienced at sea was necessary to clear his head and figure out a way forward for his beleaguered Firestorm operation. Too much was at stake to simply disappear, even though that would've been Blunt's preference. With more than sufficient funds to live out the rest of his days at sea, he could've given the world a figurative middle finger and enjoyed his retirement. It wouldn't have been how he always imagined it, but he'd be alive and left alone. And those were two things he couldn't complain about if he considered how much of an agitator he'd been among some of the world's most powerful people. Despite his attempts to vanish, his enemies might still try to kill simply because they could.

However, if Firestorm was going to be successful moving forward, it needed Brady Hawk sharp and polished. And Alex, the one who'd been responsible for keeping Hawk that way, had just indicated she was heading over to work for Searchlight.

While Searchlight was a relatively new player in the shadowy world of espionage and anti-terrorism units, Blunt had enough intelligence on it to know its agenda wasn't exactly as noble as it purported to be. Its tactics were also dirty and underhanded, even as Blunt somewhat admired their audacity. Instead of taking on Hawk head on, Searchlight opted to remove his savvy handler. Without Alex, Hawk wouldn't be able to enter into some of his missions with the confidence that someone somewhere had his back. In a profession with razor thin margins, losing such a partner could mean the difference in life and death. And without Hawk, Blunt had nothing. Firestorm would be nothing.

Blunt finished his glass and picked up his satellite phone to give Hank Munson a call. Munson served as a recruiter for the CIA years ago but had transitioned to working in the private sector once he retired. His vast network and keen eye for potentially talented agents made him a sought-after man, even though he was well into his seventies. However, it was Munson's underground connections that drove Blunt to reconnect with his old friend. Blunt needed someone to replace Alex, someone who was really good at the job. Discreet, covert, hacking skills off the chart, and off everyone's radar—they seemed like an odd combination for an employer to look for, but that was the perfect mix for an ideal candidate to replace Alex and give Hawk the help he needed.

The phone rang several times before it went to voicemail.

Blunt left a message and a callback protocol in the off chance that the CIA was listening in on Munson's phone. It wasn't likely, but Blunt wasn't taking any chances.

Blunt wondered if maybe Munson not answering was a sign. After all, it wasn't like Blunt wanted to break in another handler, no matter how potentially good the person could be. It would require much more effort and time than he wanted to invest. He'd rather woo Alex back to Firestorm. Maybe more money would do it. Pay raises worked for most people. He'd double Searchlight's offer. It's not like it would hurt Firestorm's bottom line. Or maybe she simply would accept more transparency. He could tell her what she wanted to hear if it meant getting her back and board and working with Hawk again.

After a few minutes, Blunt's phone rang again. Anticipating the call from Munson, Blunt picked up after the first ring. He was briefly disappointed when Munson's voice wasn't on the other end; instead, it was Hawk's.

"They took her, right in broad daylight," Hawk said.

"You're talking about Alex, right?" Blunt asked.

"Yeah. I couldn't believe how brazen of a kidnapping this was. Four guys surrounded her, escorted her to a van, and drove off after they forced her inside."

"And it looked like a kidnapping?"

"She looked like she was complying because she had no other choice."

Blunt picked his glass up and flung it into the water.

"Damn it! This is my fault. I shouldn't have sat on my hands about this for so long."

"As much as I hate it, you can't blame yourself. She's a grown woman and makes her own decisions."

"But she's making a very bad decision, just like her mother. I swore I wouldn't let this happen to her."

"Her mother? What happened with her mother?"

Blunt sighed. "Look, I don't want to get into that right now. Let's stay focused here. We need to get her back ASAP."

"How does this affect the mission to save Abbadi?"

"I don't see how you can do this without her, but if I don't have another handler in place by tomorrow, you'll still need to travel to Prague and take care of it on your own. Think you can handle it?"

"If it's as important as you say it is, I'll figure out a way."

"Good. Now, one more question: Do you think it was Searchlight that took her?"

"She told me she was waiting for them to make contact, so I don't know who else it could be."

Blunt stared at the horizon, still devoid of anything but slow rolling waves.

"And they'd *contact* her by *kidnapping* her? Are you sure you're not letting your feelings for her get in the way of how things looked."

"I saw what I saw. I'd just spoken with Alex. She'd said her good-byes, but I don't know. It just seemed off to me."

"Maybe it wasn't Searchlight. Perhaps some other group has a beef with her."

"Their whole recruitment of her has been very

contrived, if you ask me. And as private of a person as Alex is, I couldn't see her getting mixed up with anyone else."

"You don't know her whole past, do you?"

"Care to enlighten me?"

Blunt hobbled down the steps into the galley to get another scotch glass.

"Not at the moment. But if you think this is solely the work of Searchlight, I might be able to help."

CHAPTER 4

Washington, D.C.

THIN BEAMS OF LIGHT slipped through the scant cracks in the door to the holding room, which felt more like a prison to Alex. She glanced at the bindings holding her ankles together. A similar tie wrapped around her wrists also constricted her hands.

If this is how Searchlight treats someone they're recruiting, I'd hate to see how they treat their enemies.

Several hours before she'd been so convinced that Searchlight was a better place to put her tech skills to use that she walked away from the best operative she ever worked with. And for *this*? She'd only regained consciousness a half hour ago.

I hope this is some kind of vetting process.

Alex tried to assess her surroundings and see if there was any opportunity for her to cut off her bindings, maybe even surprise the next visitor. But if there were, she wasn't seeing them. The room was mostly dark, but what she could see seemed bare. The walls were smooth and barren. No chair to sit on. There wasn't even a door handle, only a steel box containing a scanner embedded into the wall next to the sole entrance and exit.

Another hour went by, and Alex didn't hear a thing other than the moans and groans of an air conditioning unit turning on and off. The silence was a deafening sound, one that only gave time for her to sit and think—and regret. She wished she could literally kick herself for basing her decision to leave Firestorm based off some gripes that seemed trivial now. Somehow, Kade Parker managed to convince her that Blunt was not who he seemed to be. Parker painted a picture for her that appeared eye-opening on the surface. However, Alex knew it was devoid of nuance, and she never gave Blunt the opportunity to explain. As good as he'd been to her, salvaging her off the CIA's trash heap, she owed Blunt that much. Let him answer then judge if he was trying to play politics and evade the question. It was a simple courtesy she should've extended to him. And now all she could do was sit and wish she had.

Alex drifted in and out of sleep for a half hour before a loud click jolted her upright. She watched as the door opened and light from the outside hallway flooded the room. A silhouetted figure filled the frame and strode slowly toward her.

"Who did this to you?" the man asked.

Alex's eyes struggled to adjust at first, but she knew that voice all too well.

It was Kade Parker.

"What's going on, Kade?" Alex asked. "This isn't exactly the welcoming party I expected when I told you I was agreeable to your terms."

Parker clipped Alex's bindings around her ankles and then her wrists before saying a word. He slipped his knife into his pocket and took a couple of steps back.

"We're very serious about our privacy here, and we had to make sure no one was following you," Parker said.

"Wait—you guys are supposed to be elite in the world of espionage and you don't know how to shake a tail?" Alex waited a beat. "Unbelievable."

"If you only knew how many times outside agencies have tried to infiltrate our ranks, you'd understand why we take such precautions. We're so good at what we do, we still remain a myth to the majority of the intelligence community."

A woman entered the room. "We're more like a legend, Kade. Get it straight."

Alex rose to her feet with the help of Parker.

"Who's this?" Alex asked.

"May I introduce you to Violet Lowry, the head of our intelligence division and your new supervisor," Parker said.

Violet offered her hand to Alex, who ignored it.

Alex chuckled for a moment, putting her hand over her mouth in an effort to keep her snickers from escaping. "What is that?" Alex asked. "Your stage name?"

Violet glared at her. "A sharp tongue? I like that. We're going to get along just fine."

Violet grabbed Alex by the arm and led her out of the room and down a short hallway, which led to a series of what appeared to be interrogation rooms. Once they stopped, Violet unlocked one of the rooms and shoved Alex inside, locking the door behind her.

Alex sat down in one of the room's two chairs, which were positioned across from each other at the table. About a minute later, Parker entered and sat in the empty chair.

"What's the meaning of all this?" Alex asked, slamming her fists on the table. "If you think I'm going to work for that woman, you're out of your mind."

Parker opened a folder and spread it out in front of him. He smiled and shook his head.

"Violet's harmless," Parker said. "She can act a

little tough at times, but trust me when I say her bark is bigger than her bite."

"Why are you treating me this way? You better start talking now or I'm walking out of here."

Parker kept his head down, eyes trained on the documents in front of him. He flipped through several pages, reading under his breath while refusing to answer Alex.

She abruptly stood up and slid the chair farther behind her with the back of her legs.

"I'm done."

She turned and stormed toward the door. Like the room she was in earlier, it had no door handle, just a steel box that contained a scanner.

"You're not going anywhere, Alex," Parker said. "Please, sit back down. We have much to discuss."

Alex turned back toward Parker and walked slowly to her seat. She dragged it across the floor, creating an agitating high-pitched sound in the process. Once she finally stopped, she sat down and interlocked her fingers, resting them in front of her on the table. She didn't speak but glared at Parker.

"Thank you," Parker said. "Now, we may begin." He rearranged his papers again, ensuring they were perfectly aligned. "We're aware of your past history with the CIA," Parker continued. "Do you care to elaborate more on what led to your dismissal?"

"If you recruited me without doing due diligence in your research of my previous employment, I definitely have no intention of working with Searchlight, so we can just end this little charade right now. I'll be out of your hair and on my way."

"Alex, of course we're aware of what happened to you. However, we wanted to give you a chance to tell us your side of the story."

Alex shook her head. "What's there to tell? I reported some shady stuff that was going on, someone didn't like it, I got fired. It's really just that simple. I was right to report it. They were wrong to fire me. Need I elaborate more?"

Parker's eyebrows shot upward, and he made a quick notation on a sheet of paper in front of him. He took a deep breath before he continued. "How familiar were you with J.D. Blunt's endgame with Firestorm? Did he make you privy to any of his future plans?"

"Future plans? You mean like the ones to systematically and skillfully remove terrorists from the face of the earth? *Those* kinds of plans? That's all we ever did."

Parker tilted his head to the side and then wagged his index finger. "Not exactly. That's certainly not the *only* thing you did, not with Blunt at the helm."

"What are you talking about?"

"I know you had questions about Blunt's true intentions, and let me just tell you that your premonitions were correct. He's far more devious than you think."

"Such as?"

"He basically created the situations for most of your team's missions to exist."

She eyed him closely. "I'm not sure I buy that."

Parker shrugged. "You can ignore facts and believe whatever you want; it's exactly what most people in the world do anyway. But take your last mission, for example. We have intel that suggests Blunt fed Al Hasib, the very organization he's supposed to be committed to destroying, information about how to obtain the schematics for the PUB-47."

"That can't be true," Alex said, waving dismissively at Parker.

"It is, and I'll be happy to show you the intel on it once you're on board."

"Once I'm *on board*? Showing that to me is about the only way I'm going to get on board."

Parker took a deep breath and exhaled slowly. "I'm afraid I can't show that to you until you agree to work with me. Protocol. I'm sure you understand."

"No, I don't," she said as she shook her head. "This whole thing is starting to seem really fishy to me all of a sudden. I'm quite certain that I don't think this is a good fit for me."

She stood up and walked to the door.

"Sit down, Alex," Parker barked. "You're been brainwashed by Blunt, and you're too damn naïve to even realize it."

"Open this door now," Alex said.

"You're not going anywhere."

She stormed back across the room toward Parker. "I said open the door."

She proceeded to grab his shirt and shake him. Parker, however, was prepared. He jammed a needle into Alex's neck, sending her staggering to the floor.

"Sleep well, Alex. Maybe when you wake up, you'll be ready to handle this simple interview process like an adult."

Alex felt the cold floor against her face while she heard Parker's Italian shoes click as he exited the room.

Then everything went dark.

***

ALEX AWOKE IN A CELL, one far less covert than the one Searchlight originally placed her in after picking her up near the National Archives. Steel bars and a back wall made of cinder block comprised her new surroundings. Other than a bed with a mattress no thicker than a slice of bread, the cell was devoid of any accoutrements.

"What's going on?" Alex yelled. "I want to talk to Kade Parker."

Nothing but the faint echo of her own voice.

She was so enraged that she didn't initially notice the woman in the cell next to her.

"It's best not to fight it," the woman said as she pointed to a scar on her face.

"Who are you?" Alex asked. "How long have you been in here?"

"Just go along with what they tell you to do. It'll make your stay here much more pleasant, believe me."

"Did they just grab you off the street, too?"

The woman slowly shook her head. "It's best that we don't discuss that kind of thing in here," she said before pointing toward the ceiling. "They're watching . . . and listening."

Alex glanced upward and noticed the camera with the blinking red light on the side. Her fellow prisoner wasn't joking.

Biting her lip, Alex scanned the area. For at least fifty meters to her right, she could see nothing but cell after cell. Most of them appeared empty, but it was hard to know for sure. She slumped to the floor and leaned against the wall. Looking up again at the camera, she noticed the red light stopped flashing.

What the—?

As she stood up to examine it, a man slipped up

next to her cell and opened it.

"You need to get out of here," he said.

"Who are you?" Alex asked.

"No time for questions. Listen very closely to what I'm about to say."

Alex nodded. "Okay."

"When I open this door, I want you to go down this corridor and take the first right. Take it until it dead ends. Then, take another right. Once you reach another dead end, take a left. There will be a door at the end of that hallway that leads to the outside. From there, I trust you can find your own way home."

Alex grabbed the man's arm. "Wait. Is this some kind of test?"

"Yeah, the kind of test that if you fail, you'll eventually get killed in here—or worse."

"Or worse?" Alex asked.

"Just do exactly as I said if you want to regain your freedom. I don't have much time."

Alex nodded and started to follow the man's instructions.

She walked swiftly and stealthily down the first corridor, taking the first right as instructed. She stopped at the next dead end and turned right. However, she froze after the first two steps as she heard voices coming from the other end of the hallway. Despite everything within her telling her to keep moving forward, Alex had to look in the direction of the voices. A woman and a man were talking, engaged in what appeared to be a serious conversation. But the woman looked familiar to Alex.

No, it can't be.

Alex kept walking and then glanced over her shoulder again.

It looks just like her.

That face was burned in her memory. Alex would know it anywhere—and there was no denying who it was. The image chilled Alex. She kept walking, following the man's instructions until she hit the door to the outside.

Sunlight flooded Alex's vision. She broke into a sprint, refusing to look behind her.

CHAPTER 5

Tuesday
Washington, D.C.
Rock Creek Park

HAWK HATED WAITING almost as much as being helpless. And for the time being, he was stuck with both. It was his version of Hell. He could do nothing to help Alex, and all he could do was wait and hope that Blunt's man on the inside came through.

Hawk tried to pass his time by doing what he did every morning when he was in Washington: run. Weather permitting, he preferred to run around Rock Creek Park. The Cherry Blossoms had long since vanished, but it was still a scenic run. To make the run more interesting, he often tried to count the number of spooks also getting in their workout. The most he'd ever identified on one run was twenty-two. Fifteen minutes into this particular run, he'd already counted eight.

Despite his heightened awareness, he didn't anticipate being tapped on the shoulder from behind. When he looked over his shoulder, he stopped almost immediately.

"Alex!" he said. "What are you—?"

"Keep your voice down. I'll tell you everything. Just keep running."

"This felt like *Drishyam* to me. A lone man fighting against powerful forces with nowhere to turn."

"Still trying to woo me with a Bollywood reference, are you?"

"Whatever it takes."

"Don't worry," she said. "I'm back. And I'm not leaving again."

"What happened?"

"In a minute," she said.

They remained silent as they continued jogging until Alex tapped him on the shoulder and broke off the main path. Hawk followed her until they reached an open area. Hawk recognized it as a pro move, especially from someone who spent most of her time behind a computer screen. If anyone were following them, they'd be able to spot the person with ease.

Alex sat on a bench, and Hawk followed suit.

"What did they do to you?" Hawk asked.

"I don't really want to talk about it. For all I know, they may have injected me with some tracker, which is why I need to get a full body exam from the Firestorm doctor."

"You really think he can help you with that?"

"Blunt gave me specific instructions to go see him immediately if I'd ever been taken against my will."

Hawk sighed and looked at the ground. "I wanted to help you, but I didn't want to make a scene. Plus, I couldn't tell if you were going on your own or not."

"At first, I was. They didn't have to coerce me, just point me toward the van. But it wasn't at all like that once I got inside. They sprayed something in my face and knocked me out. I woke up and didn't know where I was. Then when Kade Parker started to question me—"

"So, he was behind this?"

"Yeah, more on that later. But when he questioned me, I felt like I was being interrogated instead of interviewed. It was like he hadn't decided if he wanted to hire me. It was infuriating."

"What did you do?"

"I threatened to walk out. That's when he injected me with something and knocked me out. The next thing I knew, I woke up in a prison cell."

"How'd you get out?"

"Some guy opened the door for me and let me

out. He gave me instructions on how to escape. It was surreal, to be honest."

"I'm glad you made it out."

"Me, too. There's something up with Searchlight, and I can promise you that it isn't good."

"Did you get any good intel while you were there?"

She shook her head. "I was either unconscious or barely coming to. I hardly got the lay of the land, though I do know where their facility is now."

"Anything else?"

"Yeah, you won't believe who I saw there as I was escaping. I almost didn't believe it myself."

"Who did you see?"

Alex took a deep breath and exhaled. "I don't know how to say this, Hawk, but I saw Emily Thornton."

CHAPTER 6

**International Waters
30 miles offshore of California**

BLUNT PULLED HIS BATHROBE tight and propped his feet up as he sat on the deck of his boat to watch the sun rise. He nursed a cup of coffee and watched the sun arise out of the east in glorious fashion. Despite all the evil in the world, viewing the dawning of a new day always gave Blunt hope. And after the past few months, he needed a heavy dose of it.

The sun had ascended fully above the water, and the smattering of clouds that had been splashed with pinks and purples had turned white when Blunt's phone rang.

"Senator Blunt?" the man on the other end asked.

"I'm sorry. Who's this?"

"Please hold the line for the President of the United States."

Blunt chuckled and hung up.

In the past, Blunt had several clashes with President Conrad Michaels over issues ranging from homeland security to entitlement programs to stimulus spending. And if President Michaels wanted to talk with Blunt, he doubted it would be a conversation he wanted to have. Not to mention Blunt had gone to great lengths to fake his own death. He was leery that anyone even knew he was alive and surmised that the caller was on a figurative fishing expedition. Or it could simply be a new iteration of the Nigerian Prince scam.

Blunt's phone rang again.

Didn't this guy get the clue?

"Senator Blunt?" the same man asked again.

"I'm sorry, but you must have the wrong number. Senator Blunt died a while back."

"According to my voice analyzer, your voice is a 99.99 percent match with the recording of Senator J.D. Blunt. So, if you're impersonating him, you're damn good. Otherwise, please hold the line for the President of the United States."

"First of all, I don't care what your machine told you, I'm not Blunt. And secondly, if President Michaels insists on talking to me regardless, he can call me direct instead of having one of his little lackeys do it for him."

Blunt hung up again. For a second, he pondered tossing the phone into the water. It was drastic, but at least he'd be completely untethered—and untraceable. But he quickly decided against it. He still needed a way to contact Hawk and stay connected with the rest of the outside world.

The phone rang again.

Blunt growled and answered. "Didn't I make myself clear—?"

"If it isn't Senator J.D. Blunt," came the voice on the other end.

Blunt recognized President Michael's almost instantly. "President Michaels. How did you get my number?"

"Never mind that. I've got some more pressing questions, starting with *just what the hell do you think you're doing, J.D.?*"

Blunt cut off the end of one of his cigars and started gnawing on it. His nervous habit demanded immediate satiation.

"I'm not sure I understand exactly what you're referring to, Mr. President?"

"You know damn well what I'm talking about. But let's cut to the chase. How are you still alive? I went to your funeral."

"Mr. President, you of all people know that not everything is as it seems. How else could you have pulled the wool over the eyes of the American people. They continue to believe that you're going to keep them safe."

"Come now, J.D. You've played this game long enough to understand that certain situations can't be nuanced politically. Sometimes, it's more about how people *feel* than the reality of the situation."

"Not when it comes to matters of national security, much less stabilizing the world's most destabilized region."

"While I agree with you on some level, J.D., the truth is real problems in this country require money. And nothing will get Americans writing checks faster than the thought of a foreign invasion or an Islamic extremist missile strike. They won't care how much they're taxed if they remain safe. It's simple math with a little bit of politics mixed in."

Blunt sipped his coffee and considered his response. "You're disgusting. You really are."

"Are you really so naïve to think that the American people know what's best for themselves? The truth is, they don't. You know and I know it. The problem is, they haven't got a clue. And it's my job, a job those same American people elected me to do, to ensure that this country continues on a track to prosperity. The biggest challenge I see is that prosperity will never happen under the current system. Everyone is fat and happy to some extent and unwilling to make the sacrifices necessary to expand and grow."

"And *you* have the answers, I suppose," Blunt said, his quip dripping with sarcasm.

"I have some of them, starting with the need to control the people more."

"And how do you intend to do that?"

"You already know the answer, J.D. The more people are scared, the more they'll give up just to feel safe. It's a beautiful thing."

"No, it's not, Mr. President. It's repulsive. You're taking the American people for a ride."

"No, you're the one taking people for a ride with your vigilante horse shit," Michaels said, his voice rising with each sentence. "And I think it's high time you return to Washington."

Blunt sighed. "Why? So I can atone for my *sins*? And all so you can make a public example out of me. No, thank you. I'll pass on that one."

"I won't ask a second time."

Blunt peered out across the horizon as he thought he saw something glimmer on the water. "Glad to hear that. I hate being bothered with frivolous phone calls like this one."

"We will find you," Michaels said.

"Don't worry. If you do happen to find me, you'll have no jurisdiction to take me in."

"Oh, I'm counting on that. That's one little fact that ought to make you very afraid."

Blunt smiled as he prepared to deliver his closing line. "Nobody in the free world will support you once they find out what you and your little cabal have been up against."

Blunt heard a faint sound, a sound that wasn't native to the natural rhythms of the surrounding ocean. He scanned the horizon again, straining to see anything. Nothing.

"Good-bye, J.D. Don't ever underestimate my reach again. It's been a pleasure knowing you."

In that moment, Blunt realized what was happening as the faint sound became more audible. It was a boat off the starboard side. Without hesitating, he dove to the ground. But he wasn't quick enough.

A bullet struck Blunt in the shoulder as he collapsed onto the deck.

CHAPTER 7

Washington, D.C.

WHEN HAWK AND ALEX REACHED the safety of Hawk's apartment, he dialed Blunt's number. Whatever strings he pulled to help get Alex to safety had worked, and they needed to let him know. Hawk waited as the phone rang and rang. After the tenth ring, Hawk hung up.

"No answer?" Alex asked.

Hawk shook his head.

"I hope he's okay," Alex said.

"You never know with Blunt. But if something is up, I'm sure he can handle himself. He always does."

"Well, we need to get a plan together to go after Searchlight."

"Whoa. Slow down. We can't just go to their headquarters and annihilate them. We need to learn more about what they're up to, not to mention why you think you saw Emily Thornton there."

Alex cocked her head to one side. "Do you not believe that was her?"

Hawk took a deep breath and slowly exhaled.

"I believe you think that's who you saw," he said. "But can you really be sure? I mean, I just have a hard time believing that after how I saw her dragged away and shot right in front of me."

"*Right* in front of you?"

"Well, not *right* in front of me, but I saw it."

"I know this news is shaking your world right now, but I promise you, I saw her alive and well. And she's part of Searchlight. Doesn't that make you want to find out what they're really about all the more?"

"Yeah, my interest is piqued but not the point that I want to die trying to find out. If we're going to infiltrate them, we need a calculated plan, one that's well thought out and resourced well. And that's not going to happen with us just brainstorming for a few minutes. I know you're itching to get back in there for payback and get some answers out of Parker, but it's true about discretion being the better part of valor."

Alex growled. "I want to make them pay."

Hawk held up his right hand. "And they will. I swear. But we have to strike back when we have everything in place to inflict maximum pain. That time is not yet upon us. Besides, we have a Jordanian prime minister to protect."

"Yaseen Abbadi?" she asked.

"That's the man. According to Blunt, Abbadi's life is in danger. Someone has a hit out on him, likely Al Hasib, as Abbadi is attempting to bring peace to the region with a treaty that includes several different neighboring nations."

"Peace is bad for business when your business is war."

"Exactly. And if peace is ever going to be achieved in that region, leaders like Abbadi must be protected so their courage and bravery can result in substantial change there."

"You really believe that, don't you?

Hawk nodded. "I might be idealistic, but I'm smart enough to know that idealism requires more than platitudes. It requires action, the kind of action I'm willing to take."

Alex slowly shook her head.

"If you're not perfect for this job, nobody is."

"Plenty of people believe like I do. I'm not unique in that way."

She smiled. "But you have the skill set necessary to take the proper action."

"I've survived so far," Hawk said with a shrug. "And I've got no intention of stopping now."

"Well, this is great and all, but I'm not sure I can be of much help. There's no way I can retrieve any of my gear from my apartment. I'm sure Searchlight is sitting on it now, if they haven't already gutted it."

"Then you'll need to come with me to Prague."

"Doesn't Blunt frown upon that?"

"Blunt will frown upon anything, but he won't care as long as we get results. We'll get much better results with you in the city helping me than on the other side of the planet."

"And you'll be able to secure the type of equipment I need there? It's not cheap either."

Hawk nodded. "I understand, but I've got a former CIA contact there who can help us get what we need. He's in private security and won't have a problem getting quick access to all your high-end gadgetry."

"And you think you can afford it?"

"Firestorm is flush with cash. All that money we got from Al Hasib in the Congo will be more than enough."

Hawk went to his bedroom and grabbed a small suitcase for Alex. He returned and handed it to her.

"You're going to need this. Go to the store and grab a few outfits, some casual ones and maybe a nice one. You never know what the mission might hold. Then meet me at the airfield in two hours. I'll notify the pilot, and we'll be wheels up three hours from now."

"Two hours for clothes shopping? Have you ever

shopped with a woman before?"

Hawk shook his head. "Why? Is that too much time?"

Alex rolled her eyes. "Like I said, you're perfect for this job. However, as a fashion expert . . . not so much."

Hawk eyed her cautiously. "I never claimed to be a fashion expert."

"Just don't quit your day job," Alex said. "Two hours at the airfield. I'll be ready."

CHAPTER 8

A countryside farmhouse
Třebotov, Czech Republic

YASEEN ABBADI ADJUSTED his red-and-white shemagh and repositioned the long tassels hanging off the side. He glanced back up at the television where the news commentator explained that a peace summit might result in some traffic delays later during the week. Abbadi stood up and walked around the living area, stopping to look outside at his security detail standing guard around the small farm villa he'd rented for the days leading up to the summit.

With all the turmoil swirling around him, Abbadi decided he needed to get out of Amman early and clear his head. The only reason he entered politics was for this moment. As long as he could remember, he wanted to live in a world full of peace, devoid of terrorism, both home grown and foreign. His proposed treaty would align several nations and give the region an opportunity to expand, perhaps even experience an economic revolution. For years, the indiscriminate bloodshed was what held everyone back. No business would consider investing in a war-torn area.

Abbadi's proposed treaty would soon change all that.

Terrorists wouldn't be able to hide any longer. Shared information would help nations policing the hinterlands. Terrorist camps would be forced underground, if they somehow remained existent. Peace would rule again while less inclined nations would attract the miscreants. At least, that was Abbadi's hope with the signed treaty. There were always plenty of places to hide in the desert, but he wanted to make sure Jordan and his neighbors weren't among them. Lebanon, Israel, Syria, Saudi Arabia, Egypt, Iraq— they couldn't be expected to guarantee the absence of terrorists, but each country could cooperatively strike back against such organizations. It was an unlikely alliance on paper, but Abbadi was close to making it a reality.

But not everyone liked it.

He opened his Quran and sought wisdom. It was a tricky proposition. He read: There is no compulsion where the religion is concerned, in V.2:256. Then he kept reading, reaching V.2:190-191: And fight in the

Way of Allah those who fight you, but transgress not the limits. Truly, Allah likes not the transgressors. And kill them wherever you find them, and turn them out from where they have turned you out. And *Al-Fitnah* is worse than killing. And fight not with them at *Al-Masjid-al-Haram* (the sanctuary at Makkah), unless they (first) fight you there. But if they attack you, then kill them. Such is the recompense of the disbelievers.

Why must you make it so difficult, Allah?

Abbadi wished for easy answers, almost as much as he wished for peace. *If everything had been more easily explained, perhaps the current situation would've never arisen,* he mused to himself.

But wishful thinking wouldn't help him move forward. However, lamenting past mistakes might help Abbadi—and all the nations involved—avoid similar missteps in the future. They had long since past time for when simple conversations would have had an opportunity to work. Now, action needed to be taken . . . and taken quickly.

Aside from his long-standing desire to simply live in a peaceful world, Abbadi's desire to see this deal come to fruition had much to do with the birth of his daughter, Fatima. Over the years, Abbadi had seen countless interviews with grieving mothers who'd lost a young child in a war-like action. A bombing, an air strike, a drone missile. The method varied, but the results remained the same: someone no longer had a child.

He recalled watching his daughter before she left for an elite boarding school in Prague. Fatima sat at the kitchen table as she sketched a portrait of her best friend. The subtle lines and beautiful shading she mimicked on paper took what could have been little more than a sweet drawing by a friend to a true work of art. She lifted her pencil off the page and smiled. When Fatima turned the paper around to show her friend, she squealed with delight.

"Can I make this my Facebook profile?" the friend asked.

Fatima nodded and smiled back, the pride shown all over her face.

Abbadi remembered the moment and used it as a catalyst to press ahead. Such enduring memories drove him even more to give his daughter a world where she could be free to be whoever she wanted to be and learn whatever she wanted to learn. She didn't need to be constricted by narrow interpretations of the Quran. An unexplored world was out there just waiting for her . . . and Abbadi couldn't wait to introduce her to it.

When he'd first expressed this desire to his wife, she wept. She had adhered to the cultural rules of the time, even though she wanted to do so much more.

And when her own husband suggested giving her permission to do things that for generations had been limited to men-only activities, she leapt at the chance.

Even such generous extensions of grace resulted in a backlash against Abbadi. The old guard wondered how King Talal II had even allowed such a man to serve at the pleasure of the people, elections or not. Abbadi had made every effort to be fair in all his dealings with all people, but he recognized he needed to possess more tact.

Looking outside the big glass window of his temporary T- ebotov farmhouse, Abbadi realized it was only a matter of time before King Talal II removed him, just as Abbadi had seen done before with other prime ministers who didn't meet the king's standard.

An idea struck Abbadi, an idea that provided a way out for him. He'd be able to keep his position, and all while helping the people. And King Talal II would think it was his idea.

Abbadi smiled and commenced to jotting down on paper what he'd found. He also checked his calendar to see that he had a special lunch date set up with Fatima for the next day. His grin grew even wider.

But it was a fleeting smile.

Abbadi's phone rang, and he picked it up. "Hello?"

"Mr. Abbadi," the man said.

"Yes," Abbadi said. "Who is this?"

"Who I am isn't important," the man said. "But what is important is that we have your daughter."

"*Fatima*," Abbadi exclaimed.

"Our demands are simple," the man said. "Dissolve the treaty later this week . . . or there will be dire consequences for your daughter. We'll be watching."

Click.

CHAPTER 9

Wednesday

Prague, Czech Republic

HAWK WATCHED AS A PEEP HOLE slid open and a pair of beady eyes pressed against the slot. A deep scar and an intricate tattoo pattern ran across the bridge of the man's nose, prompting Hawk to question his decision to reach out to the man for help. Hawk glanced at Alex, who appeared equally disturbed by the man's appearance.

"Co chceš?" the man asked.

Hawk knew enough Czech to get by.

"*Sv- tový mír,*" he said, responding with the password Blunt had given him: world peace.

A series of clicks continued for fifteen seconds until the door finally swung open.

Hawk looked up at the man, a rare event in his life. In that moment, Hawk also hoped that he never offended the man to the point that it would come to blows.

"J.D. Blunt sent us," Hawk said.

The man gestured for Hawk and Alex to hurry inside before shutting the door and re-securing all the locks. He then turned to his visitors and offered his hand.

"They call me Tiny," he said in a broken English accent.

Hawk tried to stifle a smile. He found the nickname for a man that large humorous, even though it was a practice that extended deep into the annals of history.

"It's okay to laugh," the man bellowed in his deep voice. "I know what it means."

Hawk relaxed and looked over at Alex, whose furrowed brow had vanished from her face.

"What do you need?" Tiny asked.

"We need some communication devices and a high-powered laptop," Hawk said. "And Blunt says you're the man."

A wry smile spread across Tiny's face. "Indeed, I am. Give me a minute."

Tiny disappeared into a backroom and re-emerged shortly with a laptop and a set of com links.

"Scrambling software embedded on this laptop. It will give you at least one hour," Tiny said, placing the laptop in a bag and handing it to Hawk.

Tiny proceeded to press the com link set into Hawk's hand.

"Coms will last for two days on one charge. Good luck."

Hawk nodded. "How much for all this?"

"I owe Blunt my life. Take it."

Taken aback by the statement, Hawk wasn't sure whether he should have pressed the issue. He decided to try. "Are you sure?" Hawk asked. "I know this wasn't cheap."

"It's a gift. Good luck."

Hawk wanted to find out more about Tiny's relationship with Blunt, starting with how their paths crossed. But there was another question Hawk knew would be sure to gnaw at him for a few days: How could Blunt have saved this beast of a man? And while Blunt wasn't a pushover, how was it not Tiny saving Blunt?

Hawk stopped at the door and looked back at Tiny.

"I just have one question for you," Hawk said.

Tiny shook his head and wagged his finger. "I only provide equipment, no answers."

Hawk remained undeterred. "It's just that—"

Tiny lumbered toward Hawk. "I can help with your mission, but nothing else. The less we know about each other, the better."

"Anything we should know about the Pachtuv Palace Hotel?"

Tiny shrugged. "Use the front doors to enter; exit through underground tunnels. But be careful. I heard chatter that someone was going to assassinate the prime minister from Jordan."

Hawk thanked Tiny again and exited the building. They returned to their car and headed to the Pachtuv Palace Hotel.

"What did you think about *that* guy?" Hawk asked.

"I hope he wasn't selling us down the river," Alex said.

"Why would he do that?"

"I don't know, but I wish Blunt would've told you more about him. I hate just having to trust him with my life in situations like these."

Hawk slowed the car down as they approached a red light. "It's situations like these that I implicitly trust Blunt with my life. You don't need to worry. He's not going to set some trap for us or send us to someone who might be suspect when we need help."

Alex shook her head. "Blunt's not infallible, you know? Even someone in his own organization, The Chamber, tried to take him out, and he said he had no idea it was coming. Either he's lying or he's naïve, or quite possibly both."

"Everyone gets blindsided on occasion," Hawk said with a shrug. "I never would've guessed you would even consider leaving Firestorm."

"I never *technically* left."

Hawk eased onto the gas as the light turned green. "And Al Capone technically was only guilty of tax evasion."

"Okay, okay. You win. But that still doesn't mean Tiny is who he says he is."

"Check out the laptop when we get to the hotel, and if it's not to your liking, you can resume your suspicion of Tiny. Deal?"

A half hour later, they pulled into the Pachtuv Palace Hotel, checking in under assumed names as part of the U.S. State Department security team. Alex had an easy enough time hacking the fed's database to insert their aliases into the system, almost as easy as booting out a pair of guests and taking their rooms when she hacked the hotel's reservation system.

"This ought to be a lot of fun," Alex said as she got out of the car and gazed at the old world architecture of their new home for the next few days.

Hawk also scanned the area and nodded approvingly. "Yeah, this is a really nice place." He paused for a moment. "Hopefully we won't cause any permanent damage."

"As long as we keep Abbadi safe," she said.

Once they settled into their rooms, Hawk decided to pay the hotel's security chief a little visit and warn him about what he was up against.

The nameplate on the edge of the security chief's desk read Dalek Jelinek, though Hawk wasn't sure who he was since the person's face was buried in a newspaper.

"Hello," Hawk said.

The man didn't move.

"Hello?" Hawk said again.

The man dropped the newspaper.

"Can't you see I'm reading here?" he said before burying his nose in the paper again.

Hawk nodded. "Are you Mr. Jelinek?"

"Who wants to know?" he asked, refusing to move his paper.

Hawk took a deep breath and introduced himself as his legend, a Mr. Will Roberts, serving as part of the advance security team sent by the U.S. State Department.

"We need to keep this place safe," Hawk said. "And I have it on a very good authority that it won't be unless we can make it that way."

"Are you suggesting what I think you are?"

Hawk nodded. "There's going to be an attack on your grounds, maybe even your entire hotel."

"If they come at us, we'll be ready. We pride our-selves on the tight security we provide. It's why this place is chosen for such events." Jelinek waved dismis-sively at Hawk. "Let me know if you need anything. I can assure you that my team will have this facility com-pletely secure by the time all the dignitaries start arriv-ing."

"I'm more concerned about a lurking threat that's already here," Hawk said.

"That's absurd," Jelinek said. "Now, if you'll ex-cuse me, Mr. Roberts, I still have a job to do myself."

Hawk walked backward until he reached the doorway, upon which time he stopped and looked back at Jelinek, who'd hoisted his newspaper in front of his face again.

"It won't be absurd if you are the one who gets to take all the credit for stopping a major terrorist threat that would've ended any possibility of peace."

Jelinek didn't flinch.

Hawk shook his head as he exited the room. If Jelinek didn't want to help, there was nothing Hawk could do about it, except put down the threat himself.

CHAPTER 10

South Ellwood offshore oil field

Off the coast of Central California

BLUNT GRITTED HIS TEETH while navigating his boat closer to the shore. He kept his head down and didn't move for almost an hour after he was shot other than to apply pressure to his wound. The sniper would've likely killed him in any other environment, but Blunt's premonition and choppy waters resulted in a painful injury instead.

Once he regained his strength, Blunt did whatever he could to change the appearance of his ship. He swapped out a couple of the flags and applied a special temporary sticker over the spot where *Pequod* was stenciled onto the side. Now his boat was called the *Intrepid*. He'd never had to test his craft's disguise before, but he deemed it a success when he passed a Coast Guard cruiser headed in the same direction where he came from.

However, Blunt wasn't satisfied that he'd truly outwitted anyone with his quick makeover. The operation to eliminate him was likely kept quiet, though Blunt figured the Coast Guard crew he passed had been ordered to check on an abandoned boat floating in international waters.

Blunt looked at his arm and winced at the sight of all the blood still fresh around his wound. He needed some medical attention sooner rather than later, which proved to be a challenge given the fact that his own government was trying to kill him. Once the Coast Guard reported that there was no boat at the coordinates they'd been given, an intense manhunt would commence. FBI agents would search every dock and slip along the California coast all in the name of a conjured up threat to homeland security.

There was only one place he could find refuge while he dealt with his injury: an oil platform. Many platforms contained a full-time medic to deal with potentially dangerous injuries that could result while working in the water or on the rig itself. Blunt hoped he found a sympathetic medic who could also be discreet. Once his wounds were dressed, Blunt intended to travel to Mexico and find a way to get to a country with no U.S. extradition treaty. It was a simple plan, but one he presumed he could pull off.

Blunt pulled up to the Holly platform in the

South Ellwood oil field. The rig hummed with activity, and his arrival was barely acknowledged except by one man, who appeared to be inspecting one of the cargo ships at the dock. Blunt waved and introduced himself using an alias, while the man threw Blunt a line and tethered him to the dock. The man then introduced himself as Norm Looper, the third mate on Holly.

When Blunt climbed onto the dock, he removed his hand to show Looper the reason for his unexpected visit.

"We better get you some help right away," Looper said. "Follow me."

Looper led Blunt to a small elevator shaft that took them to the main deck where the sick bay was located.

The sick bay door was open, and Looper knocked gently on the doorjamb. A bespectacled man looked up from a chart he was staring at and addressed Looper.

"Is there something I can help you with, Looper?" the man asked.

"Yes, Gordon, this man here requires some medical attention, and I was hoping you might be able to help him," Looper said.

"Is he part of the crew?" Gordon asked.

Looper shook his head. "Does that really matter? This guy has a pretty nasty flesh wound and needs your help. I won't tell anybody, and you certainly don't look like you're too busy with other patients at the moment. What do you say?"

Gordon sighed and rolled his eyes. "Oh, all right. I guess we can bend the rules in this case for Mr.—"

"Jackson. Clint Jackson."

"I'll take it from here," Gordon said, dismissing Looper.

Gordon inspected Blunt's arm. "That's quite a mess you've got there. What happened?"

"There's no way to really sugar coat this," Blunt said. "I got shot."

"What happened to the shooter?"

"He got away?"

A grin started to spread across Gordon's face. "What is a sail-by shooting?"

Blunt glared at Gordon. "You're quite the comedian."

"I'll be here all week," Gordon said with a wink. "I'll need to dig the bullet out, and then we'll get you fixed up. It looks like a fairly clean entry. No worries."

Once he finished, Gordon recommended that Blunt rest for a few hours to make sure he didn't have any other complications. Blunt didn't like the idea, but he agreed.

After Gordon left the room, Blunt fell asleep in the cot. When he awoke, he was startled to find

Looper standing over him with a needle. He was about to inject it into Blunt's arm when Blunt protested.

"What do you think you're doing?" Blunt asked.

Looper drew back. "I-I was just giving you a shot. Gordon was busy with another patient and asked me to give it to you."

"Did he, now?" Blunt said as he stood up.

Looper took a step back. "Yeah. Is there a problem with me giving you a shot?"

"There is if I didn't ask for it."

Looper glanced around the room before he lunged at Blunt with the needle. Blunt grabbed Looper's right forearm and slammed it against the corner of the table, forcing Looper to drop the needle. Blunt then delivered a pair of successive uppercuts, which sent Looper staggering back against the wall.

Blunt pinned Looper against the wall with his right arm while placing his left hand loosely around Looper's neck.

"Start talking right now," Blunt said.

"Another boat came up to our platform a half hour ago, and some guy showed me a picture of you and asked me if I'd seen you. I told him you came here a few hours ago, and he told me that I needed to bring you down to them as it was a matter of national security. And I had to do it discreetly as the crew was changing shifts, and I didn't want anyone to find out what I'd done."

"You were going to inject me with a tranquilizer?"

Looper nodded.

Blunt released Looper's neck and reached down to pick up the needle. He quickly rammed it into Looper's arm, much to the shock of Looper.

"Let's hope you were telling the truth," Blunt said.

Blunt counted to ten, and Looper collapsed to the floor.

Without any time to lose, Blunt went to the top of the platform and asked the helicopter pilot if he could give him a ride to Channel Islands National Park. Blunt realized it was risky, but far less risky than trying to drive off in his boat with some FBI or Coast Guard agent down below waiting to take him into custody. Once at the park, Blunt could hitch a ride back to the mainland with a tour guide boat and then flee the country under another alias. It wasn't the greatest plan, but it was a serviceable one considering the circumstances.

At first the pilot was reluctant, but Blunt offered the man $50K for the short trip, and that garnered a different type of reaction.

"You ready to go right now?" the pilot asked.

Blunt nodded.

"Follow me."

CHAPTER 11

A countryside farmhouse
Třebotov, Czech Republic

YASEEN ABBADI STARED AT THE WORDS he'd written on the paper in front of him. As he re-read the speech for the third time, he knew it would surely stir emotions among audience members, both those present and those watching a broadcast version of it. For reasonable people, the speech would elicit inspiring emotions, the kind that make people want to work together to change the world. For everyone else, the speech would enrage them to the point of taking unreasonable action. The prospects of the latter terrified him more than hope of the former. And as much as he wanted to ignore his detractors, he couldn't. Fatima was still captive.

If Abbadi was truly honest with himself, he wasn't even all that concerned with what might happen at the hotel. With the world watching the broadcast and some of the best security personnel on hand, he remained confident no one would be able to get to him. But whoever *they* were had already found his daughter. What he planned to say in his speech depended upon whether or not Fatima was safe by the time he stepped behind the lectern.

He remained hard on himself for selecting Prague as the location for the summit. It was a strategic move as he wanted to have the backdrop for this monumental meeting to be in a place that held better optics when it came to the rest of the world. It was also a selfish move because he wanted to see his daughter. He'd already begun to regret the recklessness of his decision, one that seemed dangerous in hindsight.

The roaring fireplace behind him crackled and popped as one of his assistants tossed another log inside.

"Have you decided what you're going to say yet?" the assistant asked.

Abbadi shook his head, struggling to hold back his tears. He shuffled his papers and glanced at the alternate speech he'd written, one where he would be announcing his resignation effectively immediately. He would cite undisclosed health issues and the desire to spend more time with his family as the cause, but everything he would say would be a lie.

He walked over to the kitchen table and opened his laptop. A picture of Fatima and her piercing hazel eyes greeted him. He sat and stared at the image for a moment. His heart sank. He had big dreams for Jordan and the surrounding region. He had even bigger dreams for Fatima. Never once did he consider the possibility that those two dreams might be put on a collision course with one another with only one destined to survive. Abbadi shook his head as he stared at Fatima's picture, struggling to believe that he even gave his actions a second thought.

Abbadi's phone buzzed, and he glanced at the screen. An unknown number.

"Hello?" Abbadi said.

"I texted you a photo of your daughter. Did you get it?" asked a man. It was the same person who'd notified Abbadi that Fatima had been taken.

Abbadi scrolled around on his phone until he found the image. It was Fatima, and she was gagged while a masked man held a knife to her throat.

"You better not harm her," Abbadi shouted.

"I won't as long as you do as you've been instructed."

The man hung up.

Abbadi shuddered at the thought of anything happening to his dear Fatima. He stood back up and strode over to the fireplace. He tossed the inspirational version of his speech into the fire, almost ashamed that he'd even written it.

Abbadi concluded he had no choice, a situation that made him hate Al Hasib all the more.

CHAPTER 12

Prague, Czech Republic

HAWK HAD JUST COMPLETED his final sweep of the Pachtuv Palace Hotel when his phone buzzed. The people who possessed his cell number consisted of a tight circle, so he was befuddled when the caller ID on his phone flashed a message of Unknown Caller.

Alex fiddled with a loose button her blouse.

"You take that call," she said. "I've got to stop by the front desk and see if they have an emergency sewing kit for me."

"You sew?" Hawk asked.

"I'm full of surprises, aren't I?" she said, patting him on the arm. "Call me when you're finished."

Hawk proceeded to walk toward the water fountain in the garden before answering the call.

"Hello," Hawk said.

"Brady Hawk? Is that you?" asked the man on the other end.

"I'm sorry. Who is this?"

"Frank Lyons, CIA. Well, former CIA now."

Hawk closed his eyes and thought, desperately trying to conjure up an image of Lyons. After a few seconds, Hawk realized it was a futile exercise. "Remind me again how we met."

"We met once at a gathering at J.D. Blunt's house. I believe he introduced you as some legend, but I knew a man with hands as quick as yours wasn't who Blunt said you were."

Hawk laughed nervously. "Did you now? What gave it away?"

"You caught another woman's champagne flute a few inches off the ground, keeping the glass from shattering on the stone patio."

"It was that obvious?"

"Yeah, I knew you were working for him or with him or whatever the hell he wanted to call it. After speaking with you for a few moments, it was evident you didn't just meet one weekend while you were working as a caddie at Templeton Heights Golf Course like he claimed."

"Golf never really was my thing."

"But killing people is, especially when it comes to removing people who are threats to our national security," Lyons said.

Hawk took a deep breath and exhaled slowly as he shrugged. "Something like that."

"I also hear you're good at finding people."

"Who keeps whispering all these lies to you?" Hawk asked, starting to get annoyed at Lyons's effusive praise.

"I have a long-time friend who sure could use your help about now if you aren't in the middle of a mission."

Hawk turned around slowly, scanning the area for any lurkers who might be trying to catch some of his conversation. He then deemed the area safe and continued with the conversation. "Did you speak with Blunt about this? I'm somewhat pre-occupied at the moment, but if you tell me what the mission is, I might consider it."

"It's about Jordanian Prime Minister Yaseen Abbadi."

Hawk's interest was piqued, though he wanted to remain careful not to give away where he was or what he was doing in case this was some twisted fishing expedition. "Go on."

"If you can't help immediately, I'm not sure it will matter much, but Abbadi's sixteen-year-old daughter Fatima has been kidnapped. And I'm afraid he's about to do something drastic if he doesn't get her back."

"How drastic?"

"I think he might resign as prime minister."

Hawk made another visual sweep of the area before continuing. "And Jordan's Joint Special Operations Command isn't getting involved? This sounds more like a job for them than me. They are one of the more elite special forces units in the world."

"Abbadi's situation is too political," Lyons said. "There are rumors that perhaps some members of the team provided information as to Fatima's whereabouts to Al Hasib. Not everyone wants him to succeed."

"I'm aware of the politics surrounding his bold leadership, but is there really this level of dissent among the king's special forces?"

"Some of my intelligence suggests that King Talal himself is behind it, wanting to publicly act as if he's tough on terror but privately act to stoke the conflict."

Hawk shook his head. "These Middle Eastern governments operate with more twists and turns than a telenovela."

"It's not that much different than our own, if we're honest about it," Lyons said.

"Okay, so if I were to theoretically take this on, can you send me any information about where Al Hasib might be holding Fatima?"

"Texting it to you now. Anything you can do to help will be appreciated by Abbadi."

Hawk hung up and scrolled through the information and mapped it out. The location was twenty kilometers east of the hotel.

He hustled back to his room before he proceeded to rap on Alex's door.

"What's going on?" she answered.

"We've got another mission."

"The night before Abbadi's big speech? Are you out of your mind?"

"Al Hasib has Abbadi's daughter, and they're blackmailing him into withdrawing from the treaty."

Alex furrowed her brow. "Who told you this?"

"One of Blunt's accomplices."

"How do you know it isn't a trap?"

"I don't until I go, but if this intel is good, tomorrow's mission won't matter much, will it? So, will you help me?"

Alex nodded. "If you need my help, I'm going with you. I wouldn't want you to walk into a trap alone."

Hawk stepped inside Alex's room and dialed Blunt's number. Hawk wanted to at least get a quick report from his boss on whether Frank Lyons could be trusted. Still no answer.

Damn it, Blunt. Where are you?

CHAPTER 13

Annapolis, Maryland

KARIF FAZIL PULLED HIS CAP low over his face
and smiled. He swirled his wine glass around and drew
it near his nose, breathing in the aroma. After gulping
down half the glass, he glanced around at the Crowne
Plaza's clientele, a mix of business professionals and
military personnel, both active and retired. Fazil wondered how they would feel if they knew they were
sharing oxygen with the United States' top enemy
combatant. He wondered if they'd detest sharing air
with him as much as he did them.

After finishing off the glass, he watched the U.S.
Navy personnel decked out in their white suits enter
and exit the building at their leisure. To Fazil, they appeared to be mocking him with their every move. He
wanted to pull out a gun and lay waste to them all.

Infidels.

Fazil smoothed out the front of the Pink Floyd t-shirt he'd donned and scanned the hotel for any high-ranking military officers. He noticed one man wearing admiral bars walk past and enter the elevator. Fazil considered leaving behind a present when he left the hotel, the kind of gift that would vanish in a cloud of smoke and leave rubble in its wake. But he decided against it. That would distract him from the real purpose of his visit: to direct the bombing of a popular Washington location.

Malik Mudin pulled out the chair across the table from Fazil and took a seat. A waiter hurried over to their table and slid a drink menu in front of Mudin.

"Would you care for something to drink?" the waiter asked.

Mudin looked at Fazil, as if to ask for permission.

Fazil nodded, almost imperceptibly.

"I'll have a scotch on the rocks," Mudin said as he handed the menu back to the waiter.

Mudin waited until the waiter left before he leaned forward and hunched over, his face only a few inches off the table. "Do you think this is a good idea?"

"Relax," Fazil said. "Everything will be fine. Drink up. Enjoy yourself."

"I'm not talking about the alcohol. I'm talking

about being out in the open like this."

"Keep your tattoos covered and your hat and sunglasses on. Facial recognition software will never flag us. You have no need to worry."

"Are you sure?"

Fazil nodded. "The fact that we are sitting out in the open will make it less likely that people will remember us as shady terrorists. We'll just be two guys having a good time. Journalists will interview people, and they'll say we seemed like nice men because, well, we are."

"We're nice men who want to eliminate the terrorist oligarchs who run this country."

The waiter returned with a glass of scotch on the rocks for Mudin and then proceeded to refill Fazil's wine glass. As quickly as he appeared, the waiter vanished.

Fazil shook his head. "No, this entire nation needs to be cleansed and assimilated. As long as the people believe they have a choice to follow whatever religion they want, they'll never whole-heartedly embrace Islam. But once they realize there truly is no choice, they'll become believers."

"But are those the kind of believers we actually want?"

"We want the kind of believers who realize that their freedom is no longer important in the sense that

Americans understand freedom," Fazil said. "What's most important is that they submit to the ways of Allah. And you're going to help with that."

Fazil raised his wine glass and clinked it with Mudin's shot glass.

A Naval office sauntered into the hotel bar and glanced around at the group of early evening customers. He shot a glance in the direction of Fazil and Mudin.

"We can't even go out for a simple drink without being scrutinized and maligned by someone," Fazil said. He banged his fist on the table. "Let's burn them all and level this city."

Mudin smiled and nodded. "Whatever it takes."

Fazil scanned the room once more as he stood up. "Let's lay waste to this hotel . . . but not until we've put this entire city and nation on high alert. Go get your thoughts. We have work to do."

CHAPTER 14

Tangier, Morocco

BLUNT'S RED-EYE FLIGHT landed a half hour before 6:00 a.m. local time. It was a brutal trip, but he needed to escape the confines of the U.S. as quickly as possible. And even in Tangier, he didn't feel as safe as he wanted to, but at least it was a place that didn't invite the CIA to conduct its business without repercussions. Yet, chief among Blunt's reasons for taking refuge in Tangier was the lack of extradition treaty between Morocco and the U.S. It also didn't hurt that one of his old friends from Congress was there on official government business.

Blunt gathered his bags and hailed a taxi, heading straight for his hotel, the Riad la Tangerina. He was due to meet Paul Robinson in the lobby at 6:30 and wanted to freshen up beforehand.

Despite being in a country that was far closer to

the Middle East than he ever cared to be, Blunt exhaled for the first time in almost two days and felt like he might be able to relax, if only for a moment. The stress that accompanied avoiding U.S. operatives on the open seas and all-out assaults on his life had taken its toll. He needed to decompress, regroup, and think. The way forward for Firestorm wouldn't be easy, but it wasn't a duty he felt like he could shirk. The consequences were too dire if The Chamber managed to co-opt key world leaders to do its bidding. Searchlight's agenda, while still fully unknown to Blunt, also left him stricken with fear. He never desired to play God, yet he still felt ob-ligated to do battle with the devil.

The Riad la Tangerina staff led Blunt up to the veranda on the roof, which yielded a breathtaking view of the Mediterranean. Situated on the tallest peak on the Medina of Tangier, the hotel with its five-star staff and amenities had no equal in the city. Its privacy was also the main reason Blunt selected it for his stay, one that for the time being had no time limit.

He sat down at a table for two and took a deep breath. Before he could do anything else, one of the waiters overturned his cup and filled it with mint tea. Blunt closed his eyes and wrapped his hands around the mug, inhaling in the sweet aroma.

"I can't get enough of that smell either," said a man.

Blunt opened his eyes and looked up to see his friend Christopher Roland hovering over him. Blunt served with Roland on the U.S. Senate Committee on Foreign Relations and took numerous trips abroad to meet with foreign dignitaries. Morocco was a pleasant anomaly among the war-torn, chest-thumping Middle East political environment. They always found Moroccan President Abdelilah Benkirane to be both affable and amicable during their visits. He also vowed to give them a safe haven if they ever needed it.

Blunt smiled and gestured for Roland to take a seat across from him. "It's the best, isn't it?"

Roland nodded as he removed his fedora and placed it on the table. He shoved his briefcase beneath the table and leaned forward.

"You look pretty good for a dead man," Roland said.

Blunt broke into a slight grin. "How was my funeral?"

"I almost cried, you bastard. Don't ever do that to me again, okay?"

"Next time, it'll be for real, though nobody will be able to mourn at a funeral service."

"Is there reason for you to think someone knows you're alive now and is trying to kill you?"

Blunt shook his head and laughed as he began rolling up his sleeve to show off his latest bullet wound. "Your boss, President Michaels—he knows I'm alive," Blunt said as he pointed to the wound, which was fully exposed. "Sent some special ops sniper after me in international waters, which I believe is attempted murder. Not that anyone would believe me."

"Is Firestorm still operational?"

Blunt nodded. "For all anyone else knows, Brady Hawk is now taking orders from General Johnson and concentrating his efforts on stopping Al Hasib. Not even the President wants to shut that down."

"So, what else are you up to that has Michaels nervous?"

"There is a lot going on right now, but it probably has to do with his connections to The Chamber cabal."

Roland studied Blunt carefully. "Weren't you part of The Chamber at one time?"

"I was. At one time, it had a noble mission. But now it's corrupt, comprised of men and women whose thirst for power will likely never be quenched. I wouldn't be surprised if the entire organization started trying to kill its own."

"Is that what they tried to do to you?"

Blunt nodded. "It's why I faked my death. I needed them to believe that I was gone so they'd stop making a run at me." He took a sip of his tea. "I never imagined I'd also be afraid of my own government."

Roland dug out a cell phone from his briefcase and placed it on the table. He pushed the phone forward, sliding it to Blunt. "This is for you," Roland said. "If you ever need to reach me for any reason, use it. My special number is programmed into this phone. It's for emergency only, but at least you have it."

Blunt picked up the phone and put it in his pocket. "I hope I never have to use it."

"Me, too."

"But I'm sure that's just a pipe dream. With Michaels intent on killing me, I'm gonna have to be damn careful, that's for sure."

"I guess you're going to find out if Benkirane was just giving us lip service about offering us refuge in Morocco should we ever need it," Roland said.

Blunt laughed nervously. "When I meet with him, I'm putting my life in his hands."

"When are you going to meet with him?"

"Soon. I just want to get settled for now before I schedule anything."

Roland nodded. "Makes sense," he said before taking a sip of his tea. He took a deep breath before continuing. "So, do you have Hawk on a mission right now?"

"He's supposed to be protecting Abbadi at a summit in Prague today, but I haven't spoken with him in a couple of days."

"Pull him," Roland said in a direct tone.

"Excuse me?"

"I said *pull him*. Get him out of there. We need him to help us with another threat on our own soil."

Blunt cocked his head to one side. "Are you suggesting that we just let Abbadi die?"

Roland leaned forward and spoke in a hushed tone. "Look, J.D., I know you think Hawk's mission is a noble one, probably like all of the other ones you task him with, but there's some serious shit about to go down, and our own government is letting it happen."

"Are you saying Michaels is inviting a domestic terror attack?"

Roland nodded. "Not only that, but thousands of people will die if someone doesn't stop it."

"And you think Hawk can do that?"

"He's better than anyone we could possibly put on the case right now. And he knows the psyche of Al Hasib operatives better than anybody."

"You're sure Al Hasib is plotting this attack?"

"Positive."

"Any intel on the attack, like when it's supposed to happen or where?"

"Not yet, but that's why it'd be nice to get him in Washington as soon as possible."

"I'm reticent to let Abbadi twist in the wind like that. He's been—"

"Such a good ally to the U.S. *Blah, blah, blah.* It won't matter what he's done or who he's aligned with if Al Hasib kills ten times more Americans this weekend than we lost on 9/11. It will give Michaels the power he's been craving as the people will willingly allow him to clamp down in whatever way he convinces the public will help keep us more secure. It'll also inspire more extremists to join Al Hasib's fight. I don't think you want either one of those outcomes, do you?"

"That's not what I would prefer," Blunt said.

Roland glanced at his watch and withdrew for a moment. "Whoa. I've really gotta get going, J.D.," he said. "I'll send you all the intel we've got so you can pass it along to Hawk. Promise me you'll pull him, okay?"

Blunt nodded in agreement. "Consider it done."

"Excellent. I'll be in touch once this whole thing dies down."

Blunt watched Roland stand up, slap a twenty-dollar bill on the table, push his chair in, and walk toward the exit without looking back.

Blunt picked up his phone to call Hawk before a nagging thought started rattling around in his brain. *What if Roland is playing me?*

It was a legitimate question, yet one he didn't have time to fully parse given the gloomy fate that awaited the U.S., if Roland was to be believed. Perhaps he was simply a covert surrogate for someone in the CIA who wanted Abbadi dead. Blunt couldn't trust anyone, even someone like Roland who seemed to be his friend.

Blunt picked up his phone and tried to call Hawk again. No answer.

He stood up from the table and noticed Roland had left his briefcase.

Blunt stooped to pick it up but stopped. He had a sinking feeling in his gut that something was up. He sat there for a second, pondering what to do.

Why did Roland leave his briefcase behind? Maybe he was just in a hurry. Or maybe he put a bomb inside that was intended to kill me.

Before Blunt decided his next course of action, he heard rapid footfalls coming toward him. He looked up to see Roland.

He knelt down and grabbed his briefcase out from underneath the table.

"Got so distracted I almost forgot this," Roland said, holding up his briefcase. "Gotta run."

Blunt watched as his friend disappeared a second time, feeling disgusted that he'd even considered Roland might have tried to kill him. The paranoia was real—and Blunt wasn't sure it would ever go away. Not as long as The Chamber existed. Not as long as

Searchlight existed. Not as long as President Michaels and his cronies were in power in Washington.

Blunt took a deep breath as reality set in. He was never going to feel safe again, but at least he could help others feel safe.

He finished his tea and got up, admiring the view once more. He had serious work to do that required his full attention.

CHAPTER 15

Prague, Czech Republic

HAWK WEAVED IN AND OUT of the sparse traffic as he sped toward the location where Al Hasib was keeping Abbadi's daughter, Fatima. The sun had already started to peek above the horizon, casting a soft light on the landscape. As they drew nearer, the scenery changed from old historic buildings to rolling farmlands.

"Just a few hundred meters ahead on the right," Alex said.

Hawk squinted at the road. The area appeared to be more rural, dominated by fields and domesticated animals.

"You sure there's a compound out here?" Hawk asked as he stared long at the horizon.

"I'm just going by what's on this map," she said. "Don't kill the messenger."

Hawk shot her a look. "It's not your message; it's your navigating skills."

"Which are excellent, I might add," she said.

Hawk closed his eyes and slowly shook his head. He continued on for a few more minutes until Alex gave him the next direction.

"Turn by that little house on the left," she said. "It's only about a mile or so from here. I'm guessing it's just over that rise."

Once they crested the hill, a compound stood out on the left, the only structure on either side of the road for as far as they could see. It was set off from the main road down in a small valley. An unimposing dirt road wound toward the entrance, which was fortified by a steel gate. The rest of the compound was walled off with stone that Hawk gauged to be about ten feet high.

"I don't know if I like this," Hawk said.

He cut off his lights and turned onto the dirt road leading to the compound. There were several other buildings outside the walls, including a farmhouse and a barn.

"Park over there behind that barn," Alex said. "I can monitor everything from here. Plus that loft will make a nice sniper's nest."

Hawk chuckled. "Sniper's nest? Since when did you acquire sharp shooter skills?"

"I was born with it, I guess," she said before wagging her finger at him. "And don't laugh either. You never know when my services might be required."

"If the only way for me to escape is for you to start shooting, I'd rather you just high tail it out of here and leave me alone. No use in both of us twisting in the wind if this turns out to be a botched rescue mission."

Hawk stopped behind the barn and turned off the car. He checked his clips as he geared up to head into the compound. "Do you remember the order of everything?"

Alex nodded. "Take out the power briefly then hack into the cameras to keep eyes on the combatants. Then locate Fatima."

"Once we clear that wall, you better be behind this wheel with the car fired up. Who knows what they might have inside the compound to pursue us with."

Alex shrugged. "All the satellite images I have suggest it's nothing to be concerned about."

"I never get concerned about what I can see. It's what I can't see that worries me the most."

"Well, I'll be your eyes around the majority of the compound."

Hawk nodded imperceptibly. "Let's do this."

He slipped out of his car and grabbed the rest of his gear from the trunk. Once he suited up, he kept low while he hustled toward the wall. Once he reached the base of the south wall, he stopped to double check his coms with Alex.

"Check one, two."

"Gotcha loud and clear, Hawk," she said.

"Have you hacked the power grid yet?"

"On my mark in three . . . two . . . one . . . now."

Hawk threw a grappling hook attached to a rope over the wall and pulled until he felt the hook catch on something. Quietly and quickly, he walked up the wall. Once he reached the top, he jumped down into the compound.

"I'm in," he said as he scanned the area. "Have you hacked into the security system yet?"

"Still working on it. Just lay low and give me a few seconds." She stopped talking while she furiously typed on her keyboard. "What's it look like in there? Any activity?"

"This feels like a ghost town," he said.

"Well, that's strange. Wait—the security cameras are coming online. Whoa."

"What?"

"It's even stranger now that you say you don't feel like anyone is there, because I count a dozen or so guards in various images."

"I've got a bad feeling about this," Hawk said as he continued moving forward.

"Do you want to abort?"

"It's risky either way now. If Fatima's here, I don't want to leave her behind. There's no telling what will happen to her if they think her father has contacted someone to rescue her."

"Whatever is going on, it's certainly not a hoax," Alex said. "Or if it is, it's a good one. I just found two cameras on Fatima. She's bound and gagged—and she looks scared."

"Can you tell me how to get to her?"

"I see some ambient light coming into the room from the far back wall. It looks like she's on one of the outer walls with a small window at the top. Not sure if that helps."

Hawk crouched low and scanned the outer perimeter of the main building inside the compound. There were two other structures, both of which appeared to be small utility sheds of some sort—and there wasn't a single window on either one of the buildings. "I think I know where she is."

"Do you think you can get in through that small window?"

Hawk sighed. "Not likely. I'm going to need to get in another way, but at least we know where she's located within the building."

"Gotta celebrate the small victories to get to the big ones."

"Let's just hope it's not too late."

Hawk identified a pair of guards on the door near the south entrance. He threw a rock near an oil barrel about twenty meters from the entrance, creating a diversion. Both men went to check it out.

"This seems too easy," he whispered as he hustled toward the door. It was unlocked, and he slipped inside.

As he wound his way through the corridors, he took note of several places he could exit in case he needed an alternate route.

"Alex, you're supposed to be my eyes in here, and you've been quiet. What do you see?"

"Not much of anything all of a sudden. I'm looping all the cameras right now so they can't see you, but I've got all the live cameras up on my screen, and all the guards have vanished."

Hawk finally found the door leading to Fatima's cell. A guard armed with a machine gun stood watch.

Hawk took a deep breath.

"Wish me luck," he said.

He exploded toward the door, catching the guard by surprise. Hawk put two bullets in the man—one in his chest, the other in his head—and watched him crumple to the ground. Hawk fished the keys out of the man's pocket and started trying the keys in the lock. On Hawk's third attempt, he unlocked the door and went inside. In the corner of the room, Fatima was balled up in a fetal position.

Her eyes widened and she shook her head, mumbling some unintelligible phrase that Hawk figured wasn't in English. Hawk tried to calm her down, but she continued to convulse. Once he pulled the gag out of her mouth, she couldn't talk fast enough.

"What are you doing?" she said. "They're going to catch you. We'll never get out of here alive."

"Just stick with me, and I'll get you out of here," Hawk said as he ripped through her bindings, freeing her to move about as she wished. "Keep your head down, and stay close to me. Let's go."

They hadn't even reached the door before a dozen armed guards poured into the room.

Hawk put his hands up in surrender and set his gun down on the ground.

"Damn it," he muttered.

Five guards rushed over to secure the two prisoners, while the seven remaining guards kept their guns trained on them.

"A heads up would've been nice," Hawk whispered.

"I swear they weren't anywhere until they broke into the room with the holding cell," Alex said.

"Might want to get to that nest of yours and—"

Hawk became distracted when one of the guards

kicked him in the ribs. Hawk fell to the ground, clutching his side. Another guard cocked his head and furrowed his brow as he peered at Hawk's ear. The guard said something in Arabic to the leader, who gestured for the guard to proceed.

Seconds later, the guard was digging around in Hawk's ear.

Hawk squirmed to get away from the man, but it was to no avail. Once the man finally rescued the earpiece from Hawk, the guard threw it on the ground and squashed it, grinding it into the floor.

Hawk stared at the splintered pieces of his com link.

I sure do hope Alex heard what I said.

Hawk watched as the man, who was obviously the leader of the group, picked up his phone and dialed a number.

"I warned you not to put together any rescue missions or else Fatima would pay dearly," the man said.

The man held the phone away from his ear. Positioned ten meters away, Hawk heard loud shouting coming from the other caller.

"There will be consequences."

More shouting from whom Hawk now assumed was Abbadi.

"Fatima is fine, but she won't be if you don't

meet our demands. I don't need to remind you what's at stake here."

Still more shouting.

The guard pointed a gun at Fatima and pulled the trigger, jerking his weapon to the side just in time for the bullet to harmlessly fall to the ground.

More agony from Abbadi.

"Do as we said or else the girl is going to get it. Do you understand?"

"Yes," Abbadi could be heard answering. He then let out a string of expletives, a tirade in at least three different languages.

"No, we're keeping the agent. We're hoping to make a trade with the U.S. government. Don't you worry about him. He's of no concern to you anymore."

Hawk started to laugh, exaggerating just how amused he truly felt in an effort to get his captors' attention.

"What is so funny?" the lead guard asked.

Hawk kept laughing. "You think the U.S. government is going to trade Al Hasib operatives for me? You're crazier than you look. And trust me, that's saying volumes about you."

"You better hope they open negotiations or else it will be a short stay for you. It's your only chance at staying alive. Otherwise, you won't live to see tonight's sunset."

CHAPTER 16

Tangier, Morocco

BLUNT STUDIED THE DOCUMENTS Roland sent before glancing out the hotel window. Blunt wondered why Hawk hadn't called back despite multiple attempts to reach him. The urgency of his messages should've resulted in an immediate callback.

Blunt concluded that Roland's intel on the imminent attack was porous at best. It would require connecting plenty of dots, something Hawk was far better suited for. If Blunt had to guess, he would predict the attack would happen somewhere in Washington. As to the date and time, he felt woefully inept at pinning it down based on the data provided. He needed Hawk's eyes on the intel so he could assess the threat more properly—and Blunt needed him yesterday.

His phone buzzed, vibrating across the table. He picked it up, anticipating Hawk to finally call him back.

Instead, it was another voice on the other end but a familiar one. "Hello," Blunt said.

"I thought you were supposed to be dead," the man said.

Blunt briefly contemplated hanging up but decided against it. His curiosity won out. "Thor, it's been a while."

The assassin who'd served Blunt well in the past remained quiet.

"Did you call me for any particular reason? Or did you just want to hear my voice?"

Thor grunted. "I have a reason for everything I do."

"Like your reason for refusing to carry out direct commands such as ignoring the order to kill Liam Jepsen?"

"Someone had to rein in your indiscriminate killing."

Blunt sighed. "There was nothing indiscriminate about taking Jepsen out. You knew what he was up to, and you still refused to eliminate him."

"I didn't call to talk about the past. I called to talk about the future."

"The future? I don't see much of a future for me and you as it pertains to any kind of working relationship."

"I'm talking about your future, and if you want to have one or not."

Blunt picked up his cigar off the table and gnawed on it as he contemplated his next words. "If I didn't know you better, Thor, I'd say that sounded like a threat."

Thor chuckled softly. "What do I have to do so that you understand what I said wasn't just supposed to *sound* like a threat? It was a threat."

"I suppose you're going to offer me some plan to save my life, a plan that I'll most likely loathe."

"Something like that."

Blunt tapped his foot on the floor. The longer the conversation went on, the angrier he became. "I might as well hear it before I reject it."

"That wouldn't be the wisest of moves."

"Just get on with it."

Thor exhaled loudly into the receiver. It was clear to Blunt that he was getting underneath Thor's skin. "I want you to join me."

"Join you?"

"Yes, join me . . . at Searchlight."

Blood rushed to Blunt's face. If Thor had been in front of him, Blunt would've done everything in his power to kill him. "You've betrayed me, Thor. That's unforgiveable."

"My *betrayal* is no different than those rebels who refused to bow the crown during the Revolutionary War. When you realize there's a side worth fighting for, you must turn and never look back."

"Searchlight is no honorable organization. Their agenda is one of destruction and domination."

"And yet, Firestorm *never* engaged in such tactics," Thor said, his quip dripping with sarcasm.

"Firestorm's objectives were never to influence governments and seize power. It was … *is* … simply about denying power to those organizations that think they can operate in some sphere above the law for its own gain."

"So you're doing exactly what you claim to be stopping? How noble," Thor shot back.

"There is no gain for me to be made. I'm doing this because I care about my country. I care about keeping tyrant leaders at bay."

"*You* are the type of leader the world needs to be afraid of, the kind with no accountability and a hidden agenda."

Blunt bit down hard on his cigar before pulling it out of his mouth and spitting out some of the stray tobacco bits. "I see they've brainwashed you good."

"No, I'm finally seeing the light about you and Firestorm for the first time. It sickens me what you're doing."

"And who knows what you're doing with Searchlight. But I can promise this—it's not the altruistic venture you believe it to be."

"I'll take this conversation as your official rejection of the offer to join Searchlight," Thor said.

"So, what's next? Are you gonna come after me?"

Thor broke into a laugh. "Oh, no, no, no. That would be too easy. We'd rather defrock you before we gut you."

"Just listen to yourself, will you? Do you think you're suddenly talking like a man who has joined an organization with the world's best interest at heart?"

"You're one to talk. But since we're on the topic of hearts, just know that I'm going to remove the heart of your organization before I deal with you directly. I'm going to kill Brady Hawk."

Thor hung up and Blunt growled, flinging his phone onto the bed.

Blunt had one burning question that had yet to be answered about his top operative: *Where was Brady Hawk?*

CHAPTER 17

Washington, D.C.

FAZIL CLOSELY WATCHED THE VIDEO from the body cam feed as Malik Mudin affixed several explosive devices in strategic locations. The underbelly of the structure provided a plethora of places to attach bundles of C4 beyond the sight of even the keenest of security guards. The level of access a person had to the facility determined just how much and how deadly a detonation could be. Fazil smiled as he imagined the astronomical body count.

This will make Americans forget about 9/11.

If Fazil was honest with himself, he wished he'd have thought of such an ingenious plot. Hijacking airplanes and flying them into iconic structures was a plan so evil in its scope that it escaped the realm of conceivability for American minds. Even after spending a few short days behind enemy lines, Fazil realized just how pervasive—and detrimental—the American way of thinking was in regards to peace and natural goodwill.

However, Fazil readily recognized the duplicity behind such so-called values. Americans desired peace for themselves yet cheered on state-sponsored attacks on small Middle Eastern nations. For far too long the United States had ordained themselves as the global police without any accountability. Fazil saw right through the propaganda, inspired by language designed to create a sense of fear yet assuaged by military might. For years, the American government leveraged unfounded fears about the East into a basis for pre-emptive strikes.

Fazil loathed playing into the false narrative the U.S. government had created. If the U.S. had left his people alone, he would've never felt the need to strike back. But he'd attended far too many funerals of good-hearted men and women whose lives had been cut short by the indiscriminate bombing of innocent civilians. If the Americans wanted a war, Fazil was going to bring it right to their doorstep.

Once Fazil watched Mudin secure the final explosive device, he stood up and clapped. "You will be remembered as a great man, Malik Mudin. I will make sure that the whole world knows who you are and what you've done in the name of Islam."

Fazil turned off the feed and collapsed onto his hotel bed. For a few minutes, he stared at the ceiling, reveling in the natural high he felt from being one step away from realizing his dream. Fazil sat up and grabbed the remote off the nightstand. He turned on the television and flipped through the channels until he came to ESPN. A man talked as baseball highlights rolled across the screen.

Ugh. Baseball. This must be how they torture information out of prisoners.

He flipped through more channels until he came to another sports station that was also airing baseball highlights.

Fazil stood up and addressed the television.

"You know what baseball needs? Explosions!" he said aloud before breaking into laughter.

CHAPTER 18

Prague, Czech Republic

ALEX LISTENED AS HAWK'S FEED died a few moments after he was captured. Despite moving forward without audio, Alex used Hawk's sporadic commentary and conversations as he moved through the compound to help envision the situation. She took a deep breath and tried to reorient herself. No longer did this mission require her tech skills; instead, it required her to enter operative mode if she wanted to see Hawk again, not to mention rescue Fatima.

You can do this. Just relax.

Alex remembered what Hawk had said before he left.

"If the only way for me to escape is for you to start shooting, I'd rather you just high tail it out of here and leave me alone. No use in both of us twisting in the wind if this turns out to be a botched rescue mission."

She wasn't about to leave him—or Fatima.

Alex threw a rifle over her shoulder and climbed to the barn's loft. She opened the door just enough to provide a window from which to shoot. Peering through her binoculars, she watched for a few minutes to detect the guards' movements around the facility. Once they began to repeat, she fastened a silencer onto the end of her weapon.

Setting up her gun, Alex slunk to the floor and took a prone position. Staring through the scope, she spotted her first target, waiting until he rounded the building before she pulled the trigger.

A bullet whistled through the air, striking the guard in the head. He crumpled to the ground. Alex chambered another round and waited for the next guard to appear. Over the next two minutes, she systematically shot every guard patrolling the compound as each one emerged in her field of vision.

She hustled down the ladder and sprinted across the yard. Using an empty fifty-five-gallon drum, Alex hoisted herself up and over the wall. She crept across the compound yard, glancing back and forth to make sure she was unnoticed by anyone else who might have ventured outside.

Alex snagged a communications device off one of the dead guards along with a pair of handguns, an automatic rifle, and an access card. She slipped up to the door and peeked inside, delighted that no one was readily visible. Using the keycard, she swiped it against the access pad and the door unlocked, granting her access.

She walked about thirty meters before she heard someone from the command center trying to get an update with the guards. Recognizing that her window to escape was short, she hastened down the hallway.

When she rounded the corner, she identified two armed men standing guard outside a door. Based on how far she'd traveled and her own calculations with Hawk's journey, she figured the room had to be the entrance to the holding facility.

With deft precision, she shot the two guards, hitting them with two shots each. In her ear, she could hear the man at the command post panicking over the fact that none of his guards patrolling the perimeter of the building had checked in for over five minutes. She understood why he was upset, too. Five minutes was a lifetime in personal protection detail. So much could happen during that time frame. Alex smiled because so much had already happened.

Alex stepped over the bodies of the two men and entered the room. Inside, she found Fatima and Hawk.

Instead of expressing relief, Hawk narrowed his eyes. "What are you doing, Alex?" I told you to get out of here if something happened to me. I know you heard everything."

"And that's exactly why I came," she said, working to free Fatima. She pulled a knife out of her pocket and kicked it over to Hawk.

"Who are you?" Fatima asked.

"We're the people who are going to take you to your father," Alex said.

"No, you're not," she said. "You're the people who are going to get me killed."

Fatima nodded in the direction of the door, which had just slammed shut. A guard trained his machine gun on them.

"Why are you untying her?" the man demanded as he continued to inspect Alex. "Who are you?"

Alex raised her hands in the air, dropping her gun. "I don't want any trouble. I just want to get my friend here back to her father. Understand?"

The guard nodded. "I understand, but it's not going to happen. Make another move and I'll kill you."

Alex turned around, brazenly confronting the man. "No, you won't. I'm too valuable of an asset to you."

"Perhaps you're right," the guard said. "We might be able to exchange several high value Al Hasib operatives for you. At first we only had one person, but now we have three. I love how you crazy Americans work."

Alex kept her hands in the air until she slowly

crouched to the floor and placed her gun on the ground.

"Kick it to me," the man said.

Alex followed his orders, offering no resistance whatsoever.

When the guard knelt to pick up the weapon, he glanced down for only a second. That was all Hawk needed to fire three bullets into the man and make sure he never got up again.

"Next time, please listen to me," Hawk said as he turned toward Alex.

"Save the lecture for another time," she said. "We've got to get out of here."

"Who are you people again?" Fatima asked.

"We're just some people who care about you and what your father is doing," Alex said. "Don't worry. You might not ever be as safe again as you are right now."

Hawk snatched the com link off the dead guard and inserted it into his own ear.

Alex finished freeing Fatima, and the trio prepared to venture into the hallway.

"You take the forward position," Hawk said. "I'll take the flank."

As soon as Alex was identifiable in the hallway, a bullet whizzed past her.

"Don't move," a guard yelled.

Recognizing how valuable she was to Al Hasib based on the previous guard's statements, Alex was willing to risk that the guard who'd just shot at her wasn't going to kill her.

She threw her hands in the air and kept walking. She gritted her teeth and let Hawk know about the shooter.

"Down the hall on the left, about forty meters away," she said as she kept her jaw set. Her ventriloquist act could've landed her on a night-time television talk show.

"Roger that," Hawk said.

Fatima followed Alex, both keeping their hands raised.

Meanwhile, Hawk remained behind them and out of sight. After a moment, she heard two rapid gunshots and a body hit the floor.

"Go, go, go," Hawk said as he ran after them.

Alex raced toward the exit with Fatima in tow. Once they hit the door, she heard Hawk laying down cover for them as they reached the courtyard. In a dead sprint toward the gate, she helped Fatima over and began scaling it herself. Alex led Fatima up the hill toward the barn and cover while they waited on Hawk.

Alex couldn't see inside the compound, but she scampered up into the loft to get a better view. The shooting suddenly stopped, and voices could be heard shouting. She pulled out her rifle and peered through the scope again.

Hawk had been captured by one of the guards and was being led toward a man who acted as if he was in charge.

"We don't have time for this," she muttered to herself.

She slid another bullet into the chamber and set the sights on the leader.

Wait for it. Wait for it.

She squeezed the trigger and sent a shot ripping through the air that eventually found its mark, entering through a small hole in the man's right temple and exiting in a gaping hole on the left. Alex watched as Hawk grabbed the man's gun and took out several of the surrounding guards. In a matter of seconds, he'd managed to break free and hit two more guards while he ran toward the gate.

Alex scurried down the ladder and fired up the car.

"Get in," she yelled at Fatima.

Alex waited for her valuable passenger and then spun the car around so that it was facing the road.

Come on, come on.

She handed her phone to Fatima.

"Call your father," Alex said. "I know he's been worried sick about you."

Fatima took the phone and began dialing her father's number.

"Where is he?" Alex asked aloud.

After a few moments, she spotted Hawk sprinting up the hill toward the car, while gunfire ripped through the early morning air.

She leaned across the front seat and pushed the door open.

"Get in," she yelled.

He almost dove into the car and ducked as Alex stomped her foot on the gas.

"Nice shooting," Hawk said. "I had no idea you had such good aim."

"Neither did I."

Alex tore down the long driveway until she hit the main road, her tires barking on the pavement.

"Fatima, have you reached your father yet?" she asked.

Fatima handed the phone back to Alex. "I called him three times but he hasn't answered yet."

Alex looked at Hawk. "We've got to hurry. He's supposed to speak in ninety minutes."

CHAPTER 19

Tangier, Morocco

BLUNT SCOURED NEWS WEBSITES to see if something monumental had happened somewhere in the world, namely Prague. But there hadn't been anything to appear online yet. If he were to believe the news sites, it was as if the entire world was living in peace and harmony.

What a joke.

Blunt checked his phone again. No messages. He wanted to speak with Hawk about the condition of the mission in Prague and hopefully urge him back to the states where there was apparently a real and credible threat, even if no one knew what it was yet. Still nothing from his top and only active operative.

Christopher Roland had been a big help to Blunt, even if he didn't fully trust his friend who'd been a member of the U.S. Senate Committee on Foreign

Relations. But Blunt needed someone else, someone active within the CIA to find out where the United States's espionage division was actively engaged abroad.

Blunt picked up his phone and called Mark Westin, a former U.S. Army General who had strong connections at Langley.

Maybe he knows something.

"Hello," Westin said as he answered his phone.

"General Westin, this is Senator Blunt."

Westin broke into a soft chuck. "J.D. Blunt, why I swear I thought you'd been wiped off the face of the earth. What's it been? Ten years? Fifteen?"

"Something like that."

"Well, whatever the exact time, it's been too damn long. What can I help you with?"

"I've run into some trouble and need your help."

"I don't know how much help I can be to you these days. I hardly talk to the boys over at the Pentagon, and most days I'm out fishing."

"Must be nice."

Westin laughed. "More than you know. But I'll be glad to make a few phone calls on your behalf in between baiting my hooks. What's going on?"

Blunt sighed. "I need your help in a serious way."

"Are you in trouble?"

"I'm not sure, but it sure does feel that way,"

Blunt said. "But for the record, I haven't done anything wrong."

"But what does everyone *think* you did?"

Blunt laughed nervously. "They think I'm cajoling the facts to my own benefit."

"And?"

"Of course I didn't do that. I was simply trying to help a friend," he said.

"That gives me some relief. But it never seems to be enough around this town, which seems to swing between phases of reviled enemy and mighty prosperous champion." The former general sighed. "So, what do you want me to help you do?"

"I need someone to help me figure out if I'm being played or not?"

"Played? By whom?"

Blunt chuckled. "It's easier for me to tell you who might *not* be trying to have their way with me than to list all the potential suspects. It seems like I'm always inundated with people who are after me."

"Tell me what you know."

"I know there's a potential terrorist strike on U.S. soil and nobody there knows a damn thing. I'm trying to decide if it's worth me removing my top asset in the field and sending him home to stop this bombing from happening."

"And no one at home seems interested in

helping?" Westin asked.

"Not interested in helping stop it—or simply doesn't care that it does."

"I see," Westin said before pausing.

Blunt waited, hoping that he hadn't wasted his or Westin's time.

"I might be able to help you," Westin said. "Hang tight."

Blunt waited as Westin put their call on hold. While it was no more than a couple of minutes, it felt like an eternity.

Damn it, I don't have all day. Hurry up, Westin.

No sooner than Blunt had finished thinking his less than flattering thoughts did the line come alive with the sound of Westin's gravely voice. "The intel I've seen suggests a high value target will be in the crosshairs of Al Hasib this weekend," Westin said. "And there's strong evidence to suggest Nationals Park is the focal point of the attack."

"Those bastards are going to try and blow up a baseball stadium?"

"They're going to succeed if you don't stop them," Westin said. "They've probably already planted the explosives."

"And none of your contacts is interested in stopping them?"

"Terrorism—it can create political leverage at

times," Westin said. "If this goes down like Al Hasib is planning—"

"Wait. Are you sure Al Hasib is behind this?" Blunt interrupted.

"According to this report I just got my hands on, Karif Fazil is in the Washington area and overseeing the operation."

"They know where he is, but they won't do anything about it? This is insane."

"I'm not sure they know exactly where he is, but he's been spotted around town. I wish it wasn't like this, J.D. Really, I swear."

"When will this go down?"

"It looks like it'll be Saturday."

"That's all I need to know," Blunt said before he hung up.

He immediately tried to dial Hawk again.

Still no answer. Blunt wasn't one to worry, but he was worried now. The situation was far more serious than he previously believed—and Hawk was nowhere to be found.

CHAPTER 20

Prague, Czech Republic
Pachtuv Palace Hotel

HAWK HIT THE STEERING WHEEL and let out a few expletives. Getting out of the city in the middle of the night was rather easy; returning in the thick of rush hour traffic would test any driver's patience.

"Just take it easy," Alex said. "I'm sure we'll get there before he speaks."

"What time is he scheduled to address the conference again?" Hawk asked.

"Eleven o'clock, less than an hour," Fatima said.

Hawk checked his rearview mirror and watched Fatima stare blankly at the surrounding traffic.

"How are you doing back there?" he asked.

Fatima didn't respond. She did little more than blink a few times.

"Have you ever had anything like this happen to you before?" Alex asked.

"What do you mean? Like kidnapped?" Fatima asked.

"Yeah, kidnapped or any other situation where your life was in danger," Alex said.

Hawk watched as Fatima closed her eyes and sighed.

"Well, I no longer live in Jordan with my father, if that tells you anything."

"What happened?" Hawk asked.

"I had a brother once," Fatima said, her voice quivering. "My father told him a hundred times to avoid some friends he'd hanging around. But he didn't listen. During an attempted coup, some of the same guys my brother thought were his friends turned him over to some of the militants trying to overthrow the Jordanian government. They were trying to use my brother as leverage, but it didn't work. The king was scared and wasn't sure he could trust anybody in the military, so he called on a few favors for the U.S. and asked them to destroy a known compound of the coup leader. And the drones did just that. They also killed my brother who was there, too."

Hawk exhaled slowly, burying his face in his hands. "I'm so sorry to hear that. Those kinds of stories remind me of why I'm here."

"My father was angry for a few months, first at the U.S., then at the king. But he knew it was ultimately my brother's fault for hanging around the wrong crowd he'd been warned against spending time with."

"And that's why you attend a boarding school here in Prague," Hawk said.

"My father didn't want to take chances with me making friends with the wrong people. But I guess that didn't stop the people who wanted to kidnap me. When terrorists want to kidnap someone, they'll find you no matter what."

"Well, you were brave," Alex said.

Fatima chuckled as she broke her stoic gaze. "I was scared out of my mind. You two were the brave ones. I owe you my life."

"You owe us nothing, Fatima," Hawk said. "Those men tried to take something your father valued dearly, but they failed. All we did was stop them."

"But without you, I would've—"

"It's over," Hawk said. "Try to move on and not think about the what-ifs. I would lie awake for eight hours every night, staring at the ceiling wondering how I was alive if I allowed myself to be consumed by near misses. What makes us stronger is how we put adversity behind us, yet never forgetting what it took to get through it in case it ever happens again."

She didn't say another word for the next few minutes.

When traffic started moving again, Hawk found

142 | R.J. PATTERSON

the nearest exit and attempted to navigate his way around Prague, utilizing the surface streets. The GPA app on his phone helped him avoid missing the start of Yaseen Abbadi's speech. Abbadi was pacing back and forth in the hallway just outside the hotel's ballroom where the conference was taking place.

Hawk watched as Abbadi dropped his entire speech, sending papers everywhere. Abbadi then grabbed Fatima and hugged her, pulling her tightly against his chest. The father-daughter pair broke into tears.

Hawk knelt down and collected the stray papers off the hallway floor. As he picked up the loose pages, Hawk glanced at the first few lines. "So, it is with a heavy heart today that I regret to inform you that Jordan must pull out ..." Hawk dropped his head and exhaled, exasperated over the fact that Abbadi was still kowtowing to Al Hasib's demands, even with his daughter out of harm's way and secure.

Abbadi took the papers from Hawk.

"How can I ever thank you?" Abbadi asked. "There just aren't enough words."

"Our work isn't done here yet," Hawk said. "We came to protect you while you delivered your speech, and that's what we intend to do."

"Very well then," Abbadi said with a shrug. "I'll make a few final adjustments to the script."

Hawk smiled, knowing Abbadi was likely going to revert back to his original speech.

Ten minutes later when the meeting commenced, Abbadi took his position behind the lectern, both hands gripping the sides of it and leaning slightly forward. To Hawk, he appeared to be a man who was about to unleash an attack.

But then Hawk, who sat with Alex on the front row directly in front of Abbadi, became confused as the speech the prime minister read sounded like the original one Hawk quickly perused while scooping up the pages off the floor.

"The last few days have been very trying for me personally with the kidnapping of my daughter. However, it's nothing compared to the last few years that have been trying for our entire region. We have all lost fathers and mothers, brothers and sisters, friends and acquaintances—and for what? This must stop. But it is with a heavy heart today that I regret to inform you that Jordan no longer feels bound by duty to uphold this peace treaty that I've helped draw up to bring stability to our region."

A collective gasp could be heard throughout the room, but Abbadi didn't stop.

"No, Jordan feels—and I feel—*morally* obligated to stand up to the oppressors who want us to go back to our lives of fear, lives controlled by men whose true intentions are to impose their will on the people they consider their enemies. But no longer."

The murmuring ceased.

"Today, when we sign this peace treaty, we will be joining hands and standing together to say *enough* to the terrorists who seek to control us. We will sign together as free nations because we want to remain free nations."

The room erupted in applause. Hawk looked around in awe. He noticed several men and women crying as they all applauded Abbadi. Camera's flashed and clicked around him, and a bank of television cameras in the middle of the large ballroom captured video footage of the momentous occasion.

Abbadi threw up both hands and gestured for everyone to stop. But it was a battle he couldn't win. The audience rose to their feet in a wave that spread across the room. After thirty seconds, Abbadi, whose face had flushed red, finally forced a smile.

Then Hawk saw—a tiny red dot flickering across Abbadi's chest. On instinct, Hawk leapt onto the stage and dove in front of the prime minister. The applause abruptly ended and was replaced by shouts and screams and more gunfire. Conference attendees wormed their way underneath chairs and covered their heads with their hands.

Hawk had assumed that with all the tight security

at The Pachtuv Palace hotel, the stage would be a safe place for Abbadi. Nevertheless, Hawk had scouted out the room the day before in the event of something happening during the conference. There was a door just behind the stage that was across the hall from an emergency exit stairwell.

Hawk wasted no time in rushing Abbadi out of the room and into the stairwell.

"Where are you taking me?" Abbadi asked.

"Some place safe," Hawk answered.

Abbadi took two steps up the stairs before Hawk yanked him back down.

"We're not going that way," Hawk said. "Stay with me for your own safety."

Hawk led Abbadi on a long descent into the bowels of the hotel. Once they reached a wall that appeared to be a dead end, Abbadi began to panic.

"What are we going to do now? They're going to kill us both," Abbadi said.

Hawk flashed a smile at Abbadi. "Watch this."

Hawk pushed a portion of the wall that revealed a keypad. Typing in the access code, the sealed wall opened up.

"What is this place?" Abbadi asked in awe as he stepped inside.

"It's the catacombs, where the dead are buried," Hawk said. "Prague is full of them from when

Catholicism dominated the country. And even this palace had one."

Abbadi furrowed his brow as he stared at the dimly lit and damp surroundings. "This is still far better than the alternative."

Hawk nodded. "I want you to stay here while I go out and find who did this to you. You're not going to be safe until we capture whoever was behind the shooting."

Hawk hustled back toward the door.

"Thank you, Mr. Hawk," Abbadi said.

"My pleasure, Mr. Prime Minister," Hawk said.

He exited the catacombs and typed in the code to shut the door and secure the room.

Hawk headed up the stairs and winced. He grabbed his upper right arm with his left hand and grimaced due to the pain.

In all the chaos that unfolded moments earlier, he'd been so focused on his mission of protecting Abbadi that he'd hardly noticed the bullet wound that was leaking blood.

Hawk gritted hit teeth and trudged up the stairs. He knew what he needed to do next. He needed to find Alex.

CHAPTER 21

Washington, D.C.

AS MUCH AS KARIF FAZIL enjoyed walking around in the open without anyone suspecting him, he knew it wouldn't be long before he drew a distrustful glance or two. Even though it was still considered bad form in U.S. culture to suspect an Arab man simply because of how he looked, people still did it—and law enforcement still acted on it. The *If you see something, say something* mantra that had been drummed into the minds of Americans through saturated messaging was part of the reason why Fazil felt uneasy about remaining in one place for too long. He needed a change in scenery and a place with more heightened security.

The compound Malik Mudin rented for Al Hasib activities sat just off the Potomac River in an industrial area of Washington. A brick wall about eight feet tall surrounded the property, which consisted of a large parking lot and a 50,000-square foot building three stories high in the center. A small dock provided access to the water or—as Mudin had told Fazil when he first secured the location—an emergency escape route.

There were six other operatives along with Fazil and Mudin who were there to assist in the mission. Three men would join Mudin inside the stadium to make sure that it properly imploded and all targets were destroyed. Two other men would handle the transportation needs of the group, while Fazil planned to remain at the compound with another operative to handle communications. It was a plan two years in the making ever since they saw the meeting of G-8 leaders would be held in Washington. Fazil didn't simply want to unleash a bomb to strike terror into the hearts of Americans; he wanted to make a statement. With all the leaders in attendance, they would suffer at the hands of an Al Hasib attack and realize there was nowhere they could go to escape Al Hasib's wrath.

When Fazil learned that the G-8 leaders would be attending a Nationals baseball game, he focused the entire operation on detonating a bomb at the stadium. With someone on the inside feeding him information, Fazil could have planned for any number of targets, but a baseball stadium was more than a random building. It was an American cathedral. And Fazil intended to bring it down in front of the entire nation.

With everything in place, Fazil decided his team needed to relax and enjoy themselves. He'd noticed how uptight they'd been for the past few days. Instead of sitting around and worrying if every little detail was going to go as planned, he wanted the operatives to enjoy some American delights. He ordered two dozen prostitutes and an extravagant catered meal from a steakhouse. To get the mood right, he also hired a DJ. By 11:00 p.m., the compound had turned into a raging party.

After three mixed drinks, Mudin stumbled toward Fazil.

"You know I'm married, don't you?" Mudin asked.

Fazil put his index finger to his lips. "I won't tell if you don't."

A wry grin spread across Mudin's face. He looked up at one of the women giving him a knowing look.

"Go ahead," Fazil said. "Have fun."

Fazil watched as Mudin and his new friend disappeared to another part of the building.

One of the other operatives approached Fazil.

"There's something I think you need to see," the man said.

Fazil followed the man to the window.

"Do you see that van over there?" the operative asked.

Fazil nodded.

"It pulled up about an hour ago, and it hasn't moved since."

Fazil stared out the window and contemplated his next move. "I want you to exit in one of the vans, the one that hasn't been loaded with any explosives," Fazil said. "We'll turn off all the lights, then you exit a few minutes later. That should put to rest that anything is going on here."

The man nodded and hustled downstairs.

"Quiet," Fazil said. "We need to turn the music off and the lights off for a few minutes. Does everyone understand?"

The remaining guests and Al Hasib operatives mumbled that they did.

"Good," Fazil said as he turned off the lights. The DJ followed suit, and within seconds, the raging party transformed into a setting more suited for a library.

The operative proceeded to drive out of the compound, shutting the doors to the facility behind him. There was absolutely no reason for anyone outside to stick around. But they refused to leave. And after a few minutes, they scaled the wall and approached the building.

"Everyone, silence," Fazil said. "No talking."

Cloaked in darkness, Fazil watched a pair of men

move toward the building. If they reached him, it was over for sure. If the men could catch Fazil and his operatives, the law enforcement officers would detain him for a long period of time, long enough to miss out on the opportunity to take out the G-8 leaders and Nationals Park on television.

The men crept closer toward the building, remaining hunched over as they hustled along.

"What's going on?" one of the women asked.

Fazil shot her a look and hustled toward the stairwell. He reached the roof of the building in less than a minute. He scoured the roof for something to distract the agents' attention. It didn't take long before he spotted a few rocks. Fazil proceeded to pick them up and launch them across the parking lot, over the heads of the agents.

The two men stopped and looked over their shoulders before looking at each other again. After they exchanged words, they continued on toward the building.

Fazil was taken aback by one of the women who whispered in his ear.

"I won't allow myself to be arrested by the police," she said. "If necessary, I'll give myself up and cut a deal with them."

"Ssshhh," Fazil hissed. "I'll gut you myself if you make another sound."

The woman cowered back.

Fazil glared at her and placed his index finger to his lips. He then screwed a silencer onto the end of his gun and took a shot at the van's windows. The sound of glass shattering the street made the two stop for a moment, but they kept moving toward the facility.

Unsure about what to do next, Fazil hustled down the steps back into the building and told everyone to stand against the wall so they couldn't be seen from the windows.

"We're all screwed if they catch us here," he warned.

Fazil edged near the window and peeked into the parking lot to see if he could locate the two men. Their flashlights flickered in night. They were heading straight for the building.

CHAPTER 22

Prague, Czech Republic
Pachtuv Palace Hotel

HAWK KNOCKED ON ALEX'S DOOR, begging her to let him in. The door swung open, and she motioned for him to come inside. Hawk staggered toward the bed while still clutching his right arm.

"What happened to you?" she asked while she locked the door behind him.

"I got shot while protecting Abbadi," he said.

"Is Abbadi safe?"

"For the time being, but we have to find out who did this and track them down before I'll feel safe about him going back into public again."

"Will he ever be safe again?" Alex asked.

"I doubt it, but that's the path he's chosen—and more power to him."

Alex sighed and put her hands on her hips. "So what do we do now?"

Hawk moved his left hand off his right bicep, revealing a bloody mess. "Think you can fix this?"

She nodded. "Let me get some hot washcloths, and you take your shirt off."

"You've just been waiting to tell me that, haven't you?" he said as he broke into laughter.

"Do you amuse yourself like this very often?" she fired back. "Don't flatter yourself."

Hawk grimaced as he eased off his shirt. He took a seat on the edge of the bed and waited for Alex.

"I was hoping you didn't get caught in the crossfire," he said.

"After you left with Abbadi, there wasn't any shooting," she said. "It was clear who the target was."

"Did you happen to see who the shooter was?"

"No," she called from the bathroom. "It was chaotic, and all the people shooting the event started scrambling toward the back wall. It was bizarre."

"Not everyone is cut out to be a hero," he said.

"Include me in that bunch," Alex said. "I'd prefer to sip a latte and read a book."

"Or watch a Bollywood movie?"

"That, too."

"Don't sell yourself short, Alex. I saw what you did for me just a few hours ago. We'd all prefer to sip lattes and read great literature, but sometimes we just have to do what's right and not spend all day contemplating it."

She emerged from the bathroom with several washcloths, all steaming. "Perhaps so, but a woman can dream, can't she?"

Hawk forced a smile and braced for her to apply one of the cloths to his arm. When the rag hit his skin, he let out a short scream and winced as she put pressure on the wound.

"Don't worry," she said. "It'll all be over soon."

Hawk watched her busily work to clean up his wound before digging out the bullet and stitching him up.

"I think you enjoy that far more than you should," Hawk said.

She smiled. "Did I ever tell you that my roller derby name is Nurse Pain?"

"You? You were on a roller derby team?"

"I was the best jammer we had. The Lakeside Katz Meow."

"I think I need to see pictures to believe this tale."

She shook her head. "Hopefully all pictures have been burned into oblivion."

"Why's that?" Hawk asked. "Would you be embarrassed for me to see them?"

"I volunteered that information to you, didn't I? Why would I be embarrassed about it?"

"Pictures are worth a thousand words," Hawk said. "I'm going to search for you on Google after this is all over with. You know that, don't you?"

"I'm not ashamed," she said. "However, I will bowl you over if you try to post them onto social media or show any of my friends. And I promise it won't feel good."

Hawk forced a smile. "Don't worry. I'm not interested about how I might incur the wrath of Nurse Pain. For now, I'd prefer that she help me by digging out the bullet in my arm and patching me up."

"That I can do," she said.

Hawk sat still as she wiped off a pair of tweezers again and penetrated deep into his wound to get the bullet. She dug around for a few moments, unable to get it out.

He reached into his pocket and handed her a small knife.

"Here, use this," he said. "It'll be far more painful but will get the job done."

She eyed him closely before taking the knife and opening it. In excruciating pain, Hawk gritted his teeth and refused to breathe heavily while she fished for the bullet. A few seconds later, she emerged with it. She then dashed across the room and grabbed the needle and thread off her nightstand.

"I'm so glad you know how to sew," Hawk said.

She grabbed a vial from the minibar and poured vodka over the needle.

"Don't get too excited. I said I know how to sew,

but I never said I know how to sew *well*. Just keep pressure on the wound until I can get this ready."

Hawk followed her instructions.

"I know you weren't expecting to do so much field work on this mission, but you saved my ass at the compound."

"Well, it's certainly not what I signed up for."

Hawk chuckled. "Someone wise once told me that we never get what we sign up for."

Alex smiled. "This might sting," she said before pouring vodka on the wound and then sticking the needle into his arm. She intently studied the area where the bullet had entered while crisscrossing the needle and the thread back and forth across the entrance.

"You're doing a great job," Hawk said.

"By whose standards? Yours?"

"This isn't the first time I've been shot, and I've had guys stitch me up on the field before."

"I'll take that as a compliment then."

Once she finished, Hawk gingerly rolled his sleeve down.

"So, what's our next move?" she asked.

Before Hawk could answer, he heard a knock at the door, rushed over to it and peered out into the hallway. "Who is it?"

"Ivan Dvorak, head of security at The Pachtuv Palace Hotel," the man answered.

"Just a moment," Hawk said.

He turned to Alex. "Look, that's not the head of security here. I met the guy the day we arrived, so I don't know what's going on. But I want you to stay out of sight. The last thing I want is for you to become a pawn in this twisted game."

"Why'd you even say anything?" she whispered.

Hawk nudged her toward the bathroom. "If I let him in, I have the element of surprise on my side with how I react to him. Otherwise, he kicks the door down and his guns are up and I'm in a much more hostile situation."

"That's why you're the operative and I'm—"

"Just get in the shower and wait until I call you out. Or if it sounds like he's about to shoot me, feel free to rescue me again, okay?"

Hawk shut the door before she could say another word.

"Coming," he said.

Hawk looked through the peephole again. It appeared as though the man was alone, which gave Hawk confidence that he'd be able to overpower the impostor. In a smooth motion, he flicked the chain lock off and proceeded to open the door.

As the man stepped inside, he wasn't moving fast enough for Hawk, who grabbed the man's arm and yanked him into the room. Caught off guard, the man went for his gun, but Hawk had already played out the scenario in his mind. With two swift chops on the man's forearm, Hawk knocked the gun to the ground. Then he delivered an uppercut, knocking the man out.

"Can I come out now?" Alex asked.

"No. Stay in there until I can figure out what's going. The less visible you are, the better. I still haven't decided if I'm going to let this puke live or not, and I wouldn't want him telling anyone about you."

"Fair enough."

Hawk worked quickly, utilizing bed sheets and pillowcases to serve as bindings. Once he had tied the man to a chair and positioned him sitting with his back to the wall and facing the beds, Hawk sat down and waited for him to regain consciousness.

However, he quickly took a prone position between the bed and the wall when bullets started peppering the room next door from outside. Hawk's room had been next to Alex's, and he realized those bullets were meant for him.

After a couple of minutes, the man came to.

"What's your name?" Hawk demanded, but the man said nothing.

Hawk could hear the security personnel in the hallway following lockdown protocol, knocking on one door at a time as they neared their room. Yet, Hawk wasn't convinced they weren't running the same scam the man in front of him had just run. For all he knew, they could've been the men who just rained down bullets on his room.

Based on the speed at which the men were clearing rooms, Hawk guessed they were only two doors away.

"You need to start talking now," Hawk said.

The man sighed and shook his head. "What difference does it make?" he asked. "I'm dead if I talk; I'm dead if I don't. So, I'd rather die with some of my principles still intact."

"If you were sent here to assassinate Jordanian Prime Minister Yaseen Abbadi, you have no principles."

"Sweet irony getting a lecture from you about principles," the man said. "The man who routinely defies orders and puts others at risk in doing so."

Hawk narrowed his eyes. "You think you know who I am?"

"Everybody knows about the great Brady Hawk … and his treasonous acts against the United States government."

"Treasonous?" Hawk huffed. "That's a good one. Be sure to give your script writer a raise."

"You think I'm joking?"

Hawk shook his head, eyeing the man closely. "Think *I'm* joking?"

Hawk tightened the silencer on his gun and took aim at the man's foot. The man let out a loud moan as the bullet ripped through his shoe. Fragments of leather and blood splatters dotted the floor around him.

"They're gonna hear us, you know," the man said.

Hawk shrugged. "I'm more interested in hearing what you have to say about your mission. Who are you working for? Searchlight? The Chamber? Who? My patience is running thin."

The man broke into laughter. "You really don't have a clue, do you? Sure is surprising given how they act like you're the gold standard among assassins."

"What are you talking about?"

The men's voices grew louder yet again. Hawk figured they were only one room away now.

"Getting a little nervous?" the man asked. "Well, you should be. Your little escapade here is about to come to a screeching halt, one way or another."

"If I had a nickel for every time someone told me that, I'd be doing what I'd rather be doing about now—sitting on a beach in a Pacific isle, reading a good book, and drinking bourbon. But instead, I'm stuck in here with a detestable puke who refuses to tell me what I need to know."

"I'm more or less stalling because I want to see how you intend to get out of this thing."

"Don't think you'll be around to see it."

In the hallway, doors slammed and heavy foot-falls echoed near their room. The handle moved slightly before a string of shots echoed down the hall-way. It was followed by the sound of at least three men dashing off in the direction of the gunfire.

Hawk let out a small sigh, pleased that he could focus all his attention on the incompliant prisoner.

"They'll be back," the man said, grimacing.

"Start talking," Hawk said as he remained prone.

"I can wait you out, you know."

Hawk fired another round into the man's left foot, producing the same results. "My next shot will be your knee."

The man howled in pain, twisting and turning in his seat. For a moment, Hawk thought the man might be trying to wriggle free, but Hawk knew there was no way he'd break out.

"Okay, okay," the man said. "I'll tell you what you wanna know."

Before he could utter another word, a bullet ripped through the window, shattering it. Then two more rounds promptly followed.

Hawk watched the man go limp and then lifeless. Two shots to the chest, one to the head. It was over before Hawk could get a single answer.

Crawling on his stomach, he moved forward a

few feet and reached the man's gun he'd kicked aside during their initial confrontation. As he stared at the familiar weapon, he immediately knew the man's employer—CIA.

"Crawl out on your stomach, Alex," Hawk shouted. "We're about to come under fire."

The moment the words left Hawk's mouth, another wave of shots obliterated the room. The sound of glass breaking and bullets zipping past him nearly drowned out his heavy breathing as he wormed his way toward the exit.

"You sure that's a good idea, Hawk?" Alex asked, who remained hidden in the bathroom.

"As long as you keep low, you'll be all right."

"How do you plan on opening the door?" she asked.

"Very carefully and quickly."

Hawk shimmied on his stomach to the door and then used the small nook area leading to the bathroom as a barrier. He stood up and peeked around the corner. More bullets ripped through the room.

Alex poked her head out of the door, remaining prone.

"Can you throw me that towel over there?" Hawk asked. "I've got an idea."

Alex crawled over to the towel she'd thrown on the floor a few hours before and picked it up before tossing it to Hawk. Creating a makeshift hook with the towel, he used it to latch on to the door handle out of the sight of the men who were watching Alex's room from the outside.

But that didn't stop the shooters from riddling the door with more shots.

Hawk looked at Alex. "You ready to make a run for it?"

She nodded. "Ready as I'll ever be."

"On my mark," he said.

Hawk yanked on the towel, springing the door open. He dove through the door and held it open with his foot.

More bullets pounded the door. He waited for a beat.

"Now," he said.

Alex followed him, diving into the hallway. Hawk withdrew his leg from propping the door open and scurried into the hallway. As soon as the door shut behind them, the shooting stopped.

"Okay, you can stand up now," Hawk said, "but stay low."

They both moved stealthily down the hall. Hawk reached behind him and pulled the dead man's gun out of the back of his belt. He handed the gun to Alex.

"You might need this," he said.

"Thanks," she said as she took it.

As they neared the stairwell, they heard a few men shouting at them.

"Let's move," Hawk said.

The men fired a few shots toward them before Hawk turned to shoot back, providing enough time to slip into the stairwell. The door rattled shut behind them as they raced down the steps. They descended two flights of stairs before the door above them opened.

"Against the wall," Hawk said.

Shots ricocheted off the wall nearby but all well out of danger.

They ran down another flight of stairs until they reached the bottom floor. Hawk sprinted toward the door, placing his hands on the handle. But it didn't budge.

The door was locked.

Hawk leaned against the glass to look at why the door wasn't moving. It was padlocked.

"Great," Alex said. "Now what?"

Hawk took a deep breath and tried to think as the clatter of footsteps echoed in the stairwell. They were getting closer, and Hawk had no foreseeable way out.

CHAPTER 23

Washington, D.C.

FAZIL TOOK A DEEP BREATH and exhaled slowly. He glanced around the room and could hardly see anyone else other than the people who'd plastered themselves against the wall like he'd done. Everyone else was well out of sight.

The men outside came right up to the window and pressed their faces close to the glass while they shined their flashlights inside. Fazil was certain they wouldn't see anything suspicious.

"Just looks like a bunch of vagrants having a party," one of the officers said into his radio.

"Good," crackled a woman's voice on the other end. "We've got another issue that needs your attention."

"On our way," the man said.

Fazil relaxed when the flashlight beams were directed elsewhere outside the building. He waited until he heard two car doors slam and tires screech away in the evening air before he announced that it was okay for everyone to resume their partying ways.

Malik Mudin approached Fazil and placed a drink in his hands.

"I think we could all use one of these," Mudin said.

Fazil grinned. "Nice to see you've come around."

Mudin forced a smile. "I'm not sure that I've come around, as you put it. But I am considering indulging in a few things."

Fazil grabbed Mudin's arm and pulled him toward one of the women sitting alone on the couch.

"What about her?" Fazil said as he pushed Mudin toward the woman.

Mudin resisted Fazil's shove, holding fast. "I'm still married."

"But maybe not for long," Fazil said. "And even if you were, I wouldn't tell a soul."

Mudin shook his head again and jerked his arm, freeing himself from Fazil's clutches.

"I will not dishonor my wife like that," Mudin said. "I do what I do for the advancement of the caliphate, not because I want to gain the power to do whatever I wish. People who do whatever they wish, never live happy and fulfilling lives—if they even live long at all."

Fazil sighed. "Suit yourself. I won't pressure you."

Mudin nodded. "Thank you. I need to pray now."

Without any further warning, Mudin disappeared down the hallway.

***

MALIK MUDIN slipped into a quiet room and knelt down to pray. He needed to ask for forgiveness for even thinking about partaking in the carnal pleasures provided by Fazil. Mudin tried to focus, but he couldn't find the words. The images of the scantily-clad women danced around in his mind just as they had shimmied in front of him only minutes ago.

Mudin drew a deep breath and prepared to pray, but the words escaped him. Instead of asking for Allah's help, he proceeded to wallow in his own guilt—and it bothered him. Mudin didn't want to fill his final days succumbing to the very lifestyle he loathed and wanted to eradicate from the planet. America was—and always had been—a nation full of indulgent people, people gratified in their sinful cravings no matter the cost. In his brief time there, he witnessed the first-hand effects of Americans who refused to show restraint. And it sickened him.

But Mudin was determined to go out a pure man, one who resisted temptation even as she enticed him with her most alluring vices. He was going to inflict the same level of pain on thousands of Americans that he felt when his parents were killed by a drone strike. The twisted irony was that his parents were attending the funeral of another family friend who'd been killed by another drone attack. It wasn't fair, and it wasn't right.

Mudin's father was a doctor who faithfully served five rural villages in Afghanistan. He always taught his son that peace—not violence—would be the way forward in the Middle East. Mudin recognized it was a lie. Until the U.S. government and its citizens bowed before the caliphate, the situation would never change. Seeing the decadence of the American people firsthand made Mudin angrier and more determined than ever to exact revenge for his parents' death.

He might be sending himself to the grave, but Mudin would do it with pride. His son would remember him as a man of principle, a man who sought to fight injustice in the world.

Mudin's phone buzzed, and he fished it out of his pocket. It was his son, Tabiq. Mudin could barely afford to give his son a cell phone, but in reality, he could hardly afford not to. As any caring father would, he wanted to be able to get ahold of Tabiq on a moment's notice in the event of a bombing or missile strike. Tabiq was only twelve, but Mudin knew his son understood the importance of this mission, even if he didn't fully understand the implications of what it meant: Tabiq would grow up fatherless.

Mudin stared at Tabiq and his toothy grin glowing on the smartphone screen. Mudin wanted to talk, but he couldn't. His son would understand one day.

Mudin turned the phone off, sending Tabiq's call straight to voicemail while wondering if he was doing the right thing.

CHAPTER 24

Prague, Czech Republic

HAWK RATTLED THE DOOR several times before coming to grips with the fact that they were locked in the hotel. The security protocol resulted in a literal entrapment within the confines of the building's doors. No way in or out—at least not yet, anyway.

"Well, isn't this just dandy," Alex said.

"I'd be willing to bet they locked all the exit doors but the front is still unlocked," Hawk said.

"And that exit is probably heavily guarded, too."

"You can count on it."

"So, what do you suggest we do then, Hawk?"

"The only thing we can do—ambush the guards."

Hawk yanked a fire extinguisher off the wall and recoiled in the shadows of the stairwell.

"Is this your big plan?" Alex asked. "We're going to hit the assassin with a fire extinguisher?"

"A gunshot will attract too much attention. We have to be as discreet as possible."

"And then what?"

Hawk shrugged. "I'm making this up as I go along."

Alex winked at him. "I've got phase two all planned out. You just better knock him out in one blow."

The footfalls echoed in the stairwell as the man pursuing them continued rapidly descending the steps. As he neared them, Alex stepped back against the wall, out of sight underneath the stairs.

"Make me proud," she said.

Hawk took one last deep breath and waited until he felt it was the right moment. Unloading on the man, Hawk swung hard—and missed.

The operative ducked and tried to spin away from Hawk, who grabbed the man and held him tightly. With a firm elbow to Hawk's chest, the man ripped himself free and immediately tried to train his gun on Hawk. Hawk dove to the ground and swung the fire extinguisher at the man's kneecaps, buckling him and sending him to the floor. Hawk was about to deliver one final blow to the man's head when he fired a shot at Hawk. The bullet whizzed past, but it attracted the attention Hawk was trying so desperately to avoid.

"They're down there!" a man yelled from up above in the stairwell.

Hawk whirled and kicked the gun out of the man's hand. Stunned after losing his gun, the man turned to fight Hawk in a hand-to-hand battle. But Hawk snatched the fire extinguisher off the ground and delivered a devastating blow to the man's head. He crumpled to the ground, knocked out cold.

Hawk looked at Alex. "Time to get moving on phase two."

"Follow me," she said. Alex darted into the hallway with Hawk right behind her. She ran toward the lobby before taking a sharp left and slipping into the laundry room.

Hawk followed her and froze once he realized this destination had been Alex's end game from the beginning. "If this is your genius plan, I think we're in trouble."

Alex turned around and yanked open the dryer. She pulled out a staff polo shirt.

"Here, put this on," she said.

Hawk obeyed and slipped into the shirt.

"Now what?" he asked.

"Now, we walk through the front door without anyone hassling us."

Hawk eyed her closely. "You really think this is going to work?"

"Got any better ideas that don't involve drone strikes and missiles?"

"I'm sure this will work just fine. But be ready for a gunfight."

They both stripped and redressed in staff attire. Once they finished, Alex turned to Hawk. "You ready?"

Hawk shook his head. "This isn't going to be as easy as you think, you know?"

"It'll buy us some time, which is what we're in short supply of at the moment. Agreed?"

He nodded. "I liked it so much better when you were sitting behind a computer, telling me that some assailants were converging on my position."

She glared at him. "Where's the fun in that?"

Hawk watched as she yanked the door open and walked swiftly down the hallway. He kept pace right behind, determined not to let her get more than two yards in front of him. Right now, their survival depended upon being able to close ranks and fend off attackers. It also depended upon their ability to vanish.

As they neared the common area, Hawk wondered if Alex hadn't just conceived *and* pulled off a plan that would've garnered her respect at every FBI,

CIA, NSA, and military special ops meeting. She was resourceful and acted accordingly to give them a chance at escape. Of course, if Hawk didn't uphold his end of the bargain, he figured they might end up in a promotional video for Al Hasib.

Once they turned toward the exit, the doors slid open and they walked right into a well-lit area of the hotel courtyard.

"That's them," a man yelled.

"Stay close," Hawk said as he took off running. Hawk excelled in this type of situation, the kind most people hoped they would never have to experience.

"This isn't going to be easy," Hawk said while looking over his shoulder.

"Why? Because of the people or their guns?"

"Both," he said.

"Hold your fire," one man yelled as they stepped into the courtyard.

Hawk exhaled, relieved that he'd avoided getting riddled with bullets.

"You better get somewhere safe," one of the exterior guards said.

Hawk and Alex hustled toward a small shed near the edge of the manicured property line. Outside, the rain had dug its heels in and was dumping water on the area near them.

"Do you know how crazy this is?" Alex asked.

"Less than a week ago, I was a lowly analyst."

"And now you're not," Hawk said.

"No, now I'm not—and thanks to you, I'm still alive," she said.

Hawk laughed and shook his head. "I'm sure I had nothing to do with it, but it's clear I'm not going to be able to get you to sit behind a computer terminal from now on ... even if that's where we're all best serviced by your talents."

"But my creativity in the field?" she said. "Didn't you say my retorts only barely scratched the surface of what I was capable of doing?"

"Don't get the big head," Hawk said. "We've still got to get out of this."

"In the meantime, call Blunt. He needs to know what's going on."

Hawk shook his head. "Are you kidding? He's probably spying on us right now by tapping into closed-circuit feeds. I bet he knows exactly everything that we've said over the past few weeks."

"Well, we probably need to hear from him personally before we enter disavowing territory."

Hawk sighed. "Don't you remember that's something we have to grapple with the moment we begin any assignment for Firestorm? Nobody is ever coming to get us."

"Unless Blunt intervenes."

Hawk nodded. "True, but that's only going to happen if there are large sums of money involved."

"Okay, fine. Let's call him," she said.

Hawk pulled out his phone and dialed Blunt's number. Following the third ring, Hawk considered hanging up for good. But then he went against his better judgment and let his curiosity get the better of him.

After the fifth ring, Blunt answered.

"What do you two lunatics want?" he said, delivering his first salvo.

"You might put us more in the mad scientist category after what we did today just to get to this point."

"I'm sure it was challenging, yet here you are," Blunt said. "Obviously not challenging enough."

"We've been worried sick about you," Hawk said. "Are you okay?"

"Me? I'm the one who's been worried not knowing where you guys were or what you were doing."

"We're always where we said we're gonna be, end of discussion."

"Don't make me laugh," Blunt said. "There's something I need to talk with you about immediately."

"Oh?" Hawk said.

"Yeah, I need you to return to the U.S. immediately."

"Immediately?"

"That's what I said, isn't it?" Blunt replied.

"We've got intel that says Al Hasib operatives are planning a strike in Washington on Saturday."

"And I'm the only one who can stop it? Please, I'm a little busy right now."

"Of course you are, but I'm sure the local authorities can handle it from there and protect Abbadi."

Hawk crept upright and peered through the window into the courtyard. He saw several Czech police walking around, oblivious to a pair of gunmen hiding in the shadows.

"We're still boxed in right now," Hawk said. "Can this wait?"

"Every second you're not back home in Washington just makes your job more difficult when you get there," Blunt said. "This is serious, Hawk. And thousands of people are going to die."

"What's the target?" Hawk asked.

"Al Hasib is going to blow up Nationals stadium."

"We'll see what we can do," Hawk said. "But first things first. We've got to get out of here without being seen—and make sure Abbadi is safe."

CHAPTER 25

Tangier, Morocco

BLUNT HUNG UP WITH HAWK and wondered just how serious the Al Hasib threat was in Washington. Was it all a distraction to get him to pull Hawk so someone could take out Abbadi? Because for the time being, Hawk and Alex were the only ones standing between a team of determined assassins and the Jordanian prime minister. Blunt had mastered the art of weaving a web of deception when it came to espionage. But he started to consider the possibility that even what he knew to be true was all a lie, a lie built on the false premise that his country needed protecting. The more he thought about it, the more everything began to feel like a carefully constructed narrative to achieve some politician's end game. Whatever was going on, Blunt didn't feel good about it.

Then he received a call from one of his other operatives, code name Zeus.

"Are you on a secure line?" Zeus asked.

"Speak freely," Blunt said.

"I heard some chatter about who's behind the pending attack in Washington."

"Go on."

"Senator Adams has been working with one of the CIA's clandestine black ops teams to ensure that Al Hasib's plot to bomb Nationals Park goes off without a hitch."

"Bastards," Blunt said. "Is President Michaels involved?"

"All indications are that he is at the very least aware of the situation and has signed off on it."

"This is treason. He's going to let thousands of U.S. citizens die—and for what end? A plea to authorize more power for the government? You know he's going to blame this on what he considers constricting surveillance laws."

"And yet the laws are sufficient enough to help stop a catastrophic plot like this one," Zeus added.

"Where are you?"

"Munich. Do you want me to return to Washington?"

"It might be a good idea, but don't get involved unless I tell you to. I've got Hawk working on this as well, but I'd rather not risk losing both of my remaining operatives on this one mission."

"Even if it means thousands of people will lose their lives?"

"Thousands more will lose their lives if I have no way to stop them. I need to keep one of you safe. Consider yourself my designated survivor."

"And Thor?"

"He's chosen a different path. Don't worry about him."

"So, it's down to me and Hawk as your final two operatives."

"And Alex," Blunt said. "Don't forget about Alex."

"She's not exactly an operative."

"She's not exactly the kind of asset to sit behind the desk her whole life either. It's something I've known for quite a while now. She's just like her mother."

Blunt poured himself a drink and thought about his next move. If Hawk and Alex were going to have to fight Al Hasib's top operatives as well as the CIA, he might be sending his best agent and top handler to the slaughter. On the other hand, Thor could possibly get the job done. He wasn't quite as naturally gifted as Hawk, but he was capable.

Blunt waited another half hour before deciding what to do.

He dialed Hawk's number and waited.

"What is it now?" Hawk asked as he answered his phone. "We're kind of busy at the moment."

"I changed my mind," Blunt said. "Forget Washington for now. I've got something else for you."

"No," Hawk said. "I'm not going to sit idly by while terrorists kill thousands of people."

"It's not like that, Hawk. This is far more complicated than I initially imagined."

"I can't unhear what I've already heard. And Alex is with me. We're going back to Washington this afternoon, and we're going to stop Al Hasib."

"But, Hawk—"

"Save it, Blunt. There's no reason you can give me—other than a self-serving one—that will change my mind."

Blunt listened as the line went dead. He wanted to drive his fist through some drywall. But this was Hawk being Hawk. For better or worse, Blunt recognized this as the guy he hired through and through. And if Hawk wanted to defy orders, Blunt only had himself to blame.

***

HAWK HUNG UP and turned his attention to the matter at hand. He glanced at Alex and then looked into the backseat of their car at Abbadi, who they'd managed to sneak out of the hotel.

"We're going to take you to a safe house in the countryside," Hawk said. "From there, you'll have to find a way back to Jordan."

"And my daughter?" Abbadi asked. "Where is she?"

"I asked someone I trust to take her there. She'll be safe with you."

Hawk watched a tear roll down Abbadi's face.

"I knew it would be hard, but not this hard," Abbadi said. "It makes me wonder if it's all worth it."

"Peace is always something worth fighting for," Hawk said as he shifted gears.

"But at the cost of my own family?"

"Each man must weigh his own costs in the battle against evil. Whatever you decided, just move forward with conviction."

Abbadi didn't say another word for the rest of the ride, but Hawk could tell the Jordanian prime minister was considering his next move—and so was Hawk.

CHAPTER 26

Washington, D.C.
Dulles International Airport

SINCE HAWK HAD NEVER MET with the other Firestorm operatives in person, Thor held a distinct advantage as he stood waiting for Hawk and Alex to exit the private jet terminal. It was easier to track a target when it didn't know it was being stalked.

The lingering twilight cast a purple hue across the horizon while a cool breeze swept across the parking lot just outside the terminal doors. The screaming engines interrupted what would've otherwise been a peaceful evening for Thor. Instead, he was on assignment to eliminate Blunt's top asset.

Careful not to get made, Thor kept his distance as Hawk maneuvered the surface streets back to his secret apartment in Washington. However, it wasn't a secret to Thor, who presumed that's where they were headed. Since he had hacked all of Firestorm's files before he left, any old secrets weren't secrets at all.

He'd stolen them right out from underneath General Johnson's nose. And Searchlight held them all.

Thor rolled to a stop in a parking deck across the street, which gave him a perfect vantage point to stake out Hawk's apartment. Parking between two large SUV's, Thor remained well hidden from any curious pedestrians in search of their vehicles. He pulled out his listening device and aimed it at the window. He heard the door slam and saw the lights flicker on, and a discussion about how to stop Al Hasib's threat at Nationals Park commenced.

Thor listened intently for a half hour until Hawk opened the French doors to the balcony and invited Alex to join him. Thor then watched through his scope.

"You're inviting me to sit out here and drink a beer instead of watching a Bollywood movie? I'm shocked," she said.

"All the good movies are at my other apartment. I don't come here very often."

"Often enough to keep the fridge stocked with beer."

Craft beer? I need to fire a bullet into these two and put them out of their misery. Real Americans drink Budweiser.

Thor assembled his rifle and called his superior.

"I've tracked Hawk to his secret apartment. Both targets are on the balcony without a clue that they're being watched. I could end this now if you wanted me to. Let me know when you're ready for me to pull the trigger."

CHAPTER 27

HAWK OPENED THE DOOR to his apartment and stepped inside. He motioned for Alex to remain where she was while he swept the room first. He pulled his gun out and crept around the apartment. It was clear.

"Do you always do that when you come to your personal safe house?" Alex asked once they were both inside.

"Only since I found out the CIA has a vendetta against me."

"To be fair, I think their vendetta against you is only on account of you trying to expose their plans."

Hawk put his gun away. "When the government for the country that I love and serve is operating like this, I will do whatever it takes to unmask the immoral leaders who view human life as expendable, especially when it's all for a power grab."

"Agreed," she said, dumping her bag on the floor.

"We don't have much time, so we better get a plan together quick."

"If you were going to blow up a baseball stadium, how would you do it?"

"If I had the help of the CIA?"

Hawk bit his lip and shook his head. "This is messed up, isn't it?"

Alex nodded. "Let's stop it first, okay? Then we'll figure out a way to expose Michaels and his corrupt administration."

"I'm sure this extends much deeper than Michaels."

"You're probably right, but we've got to focus on one thing at a time. Are you with me?"

Hawk took a deep breath and exhaled slowly. "If I were going to blow up the stadium with a maximum casualty kill, I'd try to destroy the structural integrity. The giant broken slabs of concrete would do the rest. To be honest, I don't think it would take that much, just a few pounds of explosives in key locations."

"This all depends on how involved the government is with this operative. Do they know about it and are simply allowing it to happen? Or are they aiding Fazil directly?"

"I'd bank on the former. The fewer breadcrumbs, the better as it pertains to being linked with Fazil and Al Hasib. If anyone in Michaels' cabinet could be tied to Fazil in any way, I doubt all the immunity and pardons in the world would protect the President. It'd be a bloodbath."

Alex pulled out her laptop and started to make some notes. "So, let's look at this schematic of Nationals Park. If you only had a limited amount of C4 explosives, where exactly would you place it?"

Hawk studied the image closely. "Without being easily noticed?"

She nodded.

"In that case, I'd plant it in these locations," he said, pointing to various locations on the map.

"You think that'd do it?"

"That's where I'd put them."

Alex closed her laptop. "That was easy. Now we've just got to sneak you into the stadium early tomorrow without getting caught."

Hawk laughed. "That might be the most difficult part of this whole assignment." He walked over to the fridge. "How about a beer? We need to unwind and relax before tomorrow."

CHAPTER 28

MALIK MUDIN ZIPPED UP HIS backpack and threw it over the fence into the Nationals Park concourse behind center field. He'd scouted out the area plenty of times in the past, and it remained the least trafficked portion of the stadium's exterior. He watched the night patrolman disappear around the corner before he attacked the fence and clambered over it.

His hands began to sweat profusely as a flood of emotions overwhelmed him. For starters, he didn't want to get caught. He held a strong desire to complete the mission he'd trained so long for. But he also felt a sense of dread about the end of his assignment. It wasn't as if there was something else awaiting him after this, not in this life anyway. If he succeeded—or quite possibly if he didn't—the end of this job carried with it the weight of finality in so many ways.

Mudin scaled a section of the wall and slid the

first explosive into place well out of view. He flicked the switch as the radio transmitter attached to the detonator came to life, the small red light confirming that the signal was live.

As he climbed back down, he thought about his son, Tabiq. Would Tabiq be proud of his father in five years? Ten years? Or would Tabiq feel betrayed and abandoned, left to fend for himself and his mother in a vicious and cruel world? Mudin wasn't sure, which created a sense of apprehension about what he was doing. Not that it mattered. Death was imminent.

Perhaps this is all for nothing. What if there is no Allah? What if I'm simply perpetuating a cycle of violence? What if my death is meaningless?

Mudin wondered if his thoughts were original or if every jihadist wrestled with the same types of issues. There wasn't a way to find out. Those who carried out their assignments always died. Those who didn't were killed for their lack of faith and failure. At least if he went through with it, Mudin knew he'd be hailed as a hero. However, he didn't care about what everyone else thought about him, just Tabiq.

Over the next hour, Mudin moved stealthily around the park, securing the four explosive devices into place. Once he finished, he climbed back over the fence and casually walked along the sidewalk surrounding the stadium.

Mudin walked for another block before he stopped and dropped his bag on the ground. He knelt down and unzipped it, staring at the stacks of cash he'd swiped from Fazil's stash while his boss was high. Mudin doubted Fazil would even notice it was gone. But the money gave Mudin reason to pause.

There was another way. He could complete his assignment *and* see his family again. He looked at the money again and quickly calculated how much it would be. He figured out how much he needed to start over in another place, a place where he could live at peace with his family. That's all he really wanted anyway. And he wasn't sure jihad was the way.

Perhaps my fate isn't sealed.

He zipped the bag up and slung it over his shoulders. He'd have to make a decision soon. He hoped he wouldn't regret it, for both his sake and his family's.

CHAPTER 29

BLUNT THOR PEERED INTO HIS SCOPE and considered pulling the trigger without waiting for the green light from his commanding officer. It would be a risky proposition, but he figured he could ask for forgiveness later if he did. Eliminating Brady Hawk would be sweet revenge. Blunt made it clear that Thor was number two in the pecking order behind Hawk, and every time Blunt reminded Thor of that fact, it was like a dagger into his ego.

However, Thor thought better of ignoring his orders. He was still new to Searchlight, and his superior likely wouldn't stand for such rogue behavior. The reaction could go either way if he decided to not kill Hawk, though Thor wasn't sure what the big hold up was. Thor kept Hawk in his sights and relished the thought of squeezing off two rounds into him. Thor even smiled to himself when Hawk's beer bottle was directly over his heart.

I could shoot two things I despise in one shot.

Thor panned over to Alex.

So, that's what she looks like. She's even better looking than I thought.

Thor had never interacted on a mission with Alex as General Johnson made it clear that she worked exclusively with Hawk. But Thor had spoken on the phone a few times with her. He tried to picture what she looked like based off her voice—and he was pleasantly surprised.

Or maybe I'll just shoot her right in front of him. It's not like he hasn't experienced that before.

Thor set his crosshairs on Alex and lingered on her before panning back over to Hawk. But he was gone.

What the hell? Where'd he go?

Thor withdrew from the scope and strained to see what was going on. Alex went inside too.

Damn it. I can't believe this.

Thor tried to look through his scope again to see what was going on, but he couldn't see anything. The lights were out. He switched over his scope to infrared mode, but still nothing.

Over the next minute, he split his attention between the balcony and the front door. Killing them out in the open would be messy, but he'd do whatever was necessary.

The front doors to the apartment swung open and they both walked out, Hawk glancing around and checking his surroundings. Thor put his sights back on Hawk and tried to gauge how much longer before the target walked out of view.

Thor's phone buzzed, and he answered immediately.

"Do you still have them in your sights?" the man asked.

"Just say the word," Thor said.

"Stand down."

"Roger that," Thor said as he pulled away from his scope and watched Hawk and Alex disappear around the corner. "Why the change of heart?"

"We think he may still be of use to us."

Thor sighed. "How so?"

"That's above your pay grade, Thor. See you back at mission control."

I should've shot that bastard when I had the chance.

CHAPTER 30

Saturday, 9:00 a.m.
Nationals Park

HAWK TESTED HIS COM LINK and looked at his watch. The center field gates opened an hour and a half ahead of the 1:05 p.m. start time. With the New York Yankees in town for an interleague clash with the Nationals, a capacity crowd was expected. At best, Hawk figured he had less than hour to identify all the explosives, remove them, and escape without getting seen.

He donned an orange vest and carried a toolbox, flashing his credentials to the lone attendant at the gate.

"I'm here on a call about some busted pipes," Hawk said.

The attendant looked down at his clipboard and rifled through a few pages. "I don't see anything on here like that."

"Why don't you call your supervisor? I'm sure he can straighten everything out."

The man shrugged and waved Hawk inside. "No need for all that."

"Thanks, buddy," Hawk said, who slapped the man on the arm after he walked through the turnstiles.

Hawk walked about fifty meters before he spoke into his coms.

"I'm in," he said.

"Excellent," Alex said. "I'm in, too. I just got patched into the security feeds on the CCTV. So far, the coast is clear. Just a few vendors milling around here and there. You should be good to go."

Hawk slipped into the stadium and stashed his toolbox underneath a seat on the back row. He readjusted the backpack he'd been wearing beneath his work vest before he entered the stadium. The bag was necessary only to collect the explosives. It's also where he kept his weapon.

Hawk figured if he acted like he knew what he was doing, no one would hassle him, especially with the number of people already buzzing in the seating area. But the concourse remained relatively traffic free.

He slid his glasses into place, giving Alex the ability to see what he was seeing.

"Is this picture coming through for you?" he asked.

"Crystal clear," she said.

"Excellent. Now, can you help navigate me to the point where we thought one of the explosives might be?"

"Look at the aisle number for me," she said.

Hawk turned to his right and spotted the aisle numbers.

"Okay, keep walking. Go up two more sections and then start climbing."

Hawk followed her orders and found the area they identified would contain a structural weakness if destroyed. He looked around to see if anyone was watching. They weren't.

He took hold of the iron metal work and scurried up toward the logical hiding spot. Once he ascended high enough, Hawk looked around.

"Help me out here, Alex," he said. "I'm not seeing anything."

"Look up for me."

Hawk directed his gaze upward.

"Go up about ten more meters."

"Seriously?"

"I know where I'd hide it."

Hawk continued climbing and finally saw what Alex saw: a small platform off the iron that could easily hold enough of the required amount of explosives. He carefully raked it toward him.

"Jackpot," he said.

"Nice work. Be careful."

Hawk gently placed the explosives in his bag and zipped it up before beginning his descent.

"Might want to hang there for a second," Alex said. "You've got company."

Hawk looked down to see a security guard roaming the concourse beneath him.

"Keep watching for anyone else," Hawk said. "I'm going to try and slip past this guy once he moves along."

"Roger that."

Hawk watched the guard saunter along a few steps at a time. He stopped and admired the field for a few moments before continuing on. This was a pattern he repeated several times until he moved far enough away that Hawk believed he could safely get to ground without the guard spotting him.

However, Hawk didn't see the guard who'd just exited the bathroom. And neither did Alex.

"Damn it, Alex," Hawk said.

The guard drew his gun and glared at Hawk. "Keep your hands where I can see them."

Hawk obeyed the man's orders.

"I swear, I never saw him go in, Hawk. You gotta believe me," Alex pleaded over his com link.

"You mind telling me what you were doing up in

the rafters?" the guard asked.

Hawk shrugged. "No need to get crazy, mister. I was just working on a project."

The guard pursed his lips. "A project, huh? What kind of project?"

"Oh, you know, just the usual maintenance and repair type stuff."

"What's in the bag?" the guard asked, gesturing toward it with his other hand.

"Just some tools and supplies."

"Mind if I take a look?"

Hawk knew he was busted. His options boiled down to either running, which would still result in the deaths of hundreds of people later that day—and possibly becoming a prime suspect in the bombing, or bluffing his way past the guard and keeping alive his chances to remove all the explosive devices.

He chose the latter.

"I was doing an inspection up there," Hawk said, pointing upward.

The guard peeked in the bag and looked up abruptly.

"Get outta there, Hawk," said Alex, her voice obviously tense as it came through over Hawk's com link.

The guard snatched his walkie-talkie off his belt and radioed back the security office. "I need some help in the main course along the right field line. Did we have any electrician scheduled to do work in the rafters today?"

"That's a negative," a man answered.

"In that case, I need two more guards to help me apprehend a suspect I caught. I think he's got explosives."

Hawk sighed. "They're not explosives," he said, continuing his bluff. "That's how I test the structural integrity of a facility."

"This looks a lot like explosives," the guard said as he grabbed Hawk by the arm. "Let's go."

Hawk heard Alex squawking in his ear. He wanted to do what she said and run; he wanted to save himself. But he couldn't; there were too many lives at stake to draw out law enforcement on a protracted chase around Washington. Not to mention, the moment someone figured out who he was, his picture would be plastered everywhere. and he'd be unable to move about the country or anywhere else. He'd be branded a terrorist.

No, Hawk realized he had to ride out this storm and think fast on his feet.

Hawk stumbled forward as the guard yanked a zip-tie around his wrists.

"I said move," the guard ordered.

"Come on, Hawk," Alex said. "Do something."

"I am," Hawk said. "Just be patient."

"Don't get cute with me," the guard fired back. "Now, move it."

Hawk considered his next course of action—and no idea he had seemed sufficient. He began to wonder if he might have blown this assignment.

CHAPTER 31

BLUNT MUDIN WATCHED SEVERAL Yankees players hit home runs in batting practice, the ball sailing into the outfield seats where fans clambered for the souvenirs. He tugged his baseball cap down tight, shading most of his face. He came up with a workable solution, but he needed to keep a low profile.

His master plan? Oversee the demolition of the stadium as ordered. However, instead of getting close enough to the target and detonating the vest, he would remove it and set it off remotely. The components he needed to make the required adjustments didn't set off any alarms while security wanded him upon entry to the park. And even if it had, the guards would've waved him inside. Nothing about Mudin struck fear in the heart of anyone. An unassuming appearance was a trait consistent with all of Fazil's candidates for his judgment operatives.

After watching batting practice for a few minutes,

Mudin walked casually up the steps and to the concourse. He picked the lock of a service room and grabbed the suicide vest he'd stashed beneath one of the shelving units when he planted the explosive devices and went to work. He disconnected several wires and refastened them on the vest, networking the wires to a new detonator point. He had to be careful not to override the remote detonator circuit, which would signal to Fazil that he'd tinkered with the vest. If Fazil grew suspicious, Fazil was certain his leader would order the execution of Mudin's family.

Once Mudin finished, he put the vest on, satisfied that his tweaks would help him achieve the end result he wanted. Once the stadium was destroyed in the bombing, nobody would be looking for him. He'd leave his wallet somewhere with his identification, and Al Hasib would never look for him again.

Mudin prepared to exit the closet when his phone rang with a call from Fazil.

"Is everything in place?" Fazil asked.

"I'm ready."

"Excellent," Fazil said. "You're not having second thoughts, are you? It's imperative that you carry out your part of the mission, which might be the most important portion."

"I'm ready to give my life for the cause and meet Allah."

"Good, good. In case you get cold feet, don't worry. We can remotely detonate the bomb."

"I'll be proud to do it myself," Mudin said.

"We'll be watching."

Fazil hung up, and Mudin stared down at his vest. *We'll be watching?*

Mudin examined his vest and noticed a small camera that was fasted to the zipper. The camera was hardly noticeable, but once he saw it, it might as well have flashed at him every time he looked at it. His plan was thwarted before he even had a chance to enact it.

Mudin swallowed hard and stepped out into the concourse. His time was limited, and the clock was ticking.

CHAPTER 32

BLUNT HAWK WANTED TO silence Alex's voice in his ear. Instead of giving him helpful suggestions, she panicked, which only made him more nervous.

"Will you please stop?" Hawk said.

"Excuse me?" the guard said. "Do you have to go to the little boy's room?"

Hawk knew he was being mocked. "I do. Is that okay?"

The guard shrugged. "I guess so."

He led Hawk into the restroom and cut his tie.

"I'm watching you," the guard said as he took up a post in the corner.

Hawk tried to casually finger comb his hair with his hand. He looked over his shoulder at the guard before deciding to remove the com link as discreetly as possible.

"Talk to me, Hawk. Talk to—"

Alex's squawking disappeared, just like her

collected coolness had ten minutes before.

Hawk was on his own, but he needed a way to permanently unshackle himself. Every scenario he could think of was too risky or resulted in him either blowing his cover or landing on an international terrorist watch list.

Maybe Blunt can help me get out of this.

It was a fleeting thought. Blunt's promise to deny all knowledge of his operatives had been burned into Hawk's consciousness. Placing such a phone call also would jeopardize Blunt's privacy.

When Hawk finished his business, the guard zip-tied Hawk's hands again, nudging the prisoner forward.

They continued along the concourse until the guard gave him a hard shove to the left toward the security offices, which were connected to the general administrative offices. If Hawk was going to break free and make a run for it, his opportunity was dwindling by the second.

As they walked past the main area, Hawk looked up at saw Thomas Colton.

"Hey, Dad," Hawk said.

"Brady? What's going on here?" Colton said while he walked toward him.

"I'm being apprehended apparently. This guy here doesn't believe that I was assigned to work for the Nationals, and he's accusing me of trying to blow up the stadium."

"Unhand this man at once," Colton said to the guard.

"I don't think so," the guard said.

"This is my son, and he's done nothing wrong," Colton said as he leaned down and peered hard at the nameplate attached to the man's shirt. "Mr. Norman, I'll have your job by the end of the day if you don't."

Norman rolled his eyes. "Whatever." He cut Hawk free and turned around immediately to head back out the door.

"My backpack?" Hawk said.

"Catch," Norman said just before he tossed the bag at Hawk.

Colton waited until the guard left before he turned to Hawk. "Would you like to tell me what in the hell is going on right now? What was that all about?"

"What are you doing here?" Hawk asked.

"I'm entertaining some of the G-8 leaders. Now will you answer my question?"

"Al Hasib is going to blow up the stadium today. You need to get these leaders out of here."

"Blow up the stadium? Are you serious?"

Hawk shook his head. "Have you known me to joke about things like this?"

"Not really, but you'd say anything to me to save face, wouldn't you?"

"I'm not playing games right now. I've got to go finish removing the rest of the explosive devices Al Hasib has planted around the stadium quickly so that Barney Fife doesn't catch me and kill us all."

Colton cocked his head to one side. "Is it really that bad?"

"I don't lie about these things, D—Thomas."

Colton forced a smile. "You can still call me—"

"Just forget I ever said anything," Hawk said as he turned toward the door and slung his backpack over his shoulder. "And make sure those leaders never set foot in this stadium today."

"Too late for that," Colton said. "We're all eating and drinking upstairs in the VIP Lounge."

"Get them out of here … unless they all have a death wish."

"I'll do my best, but world leaders are a stubborn lot."

Hawk sighed. "Make them unstubborn, okay?"

Without a second glance, Hawk dashed out the door and started to search out the remaining explosive devices. For a moment, he considered leaving his com link out of his ear. But he knew it'd only aggravate Alex, and she was likely to enter the stadium to try to help. He relented—against his better judgment—and slid the audio device back into his ear.

"I'm out," Hawk said.

"How'd that happen?" she asked.

"Never mind. I just need you to lead me to where the other explosives are likely to be, according to the schematics."

For the next half hour, Hawk stealthily worked his way around the stadium, removing the explosives Al Hasib had put in place. Once Hawk finished, he notified Alex.

"I've got to get these explosives out of the stadium," he said.

"Dump them in the Potomac," she said.

"Good idea."

"But, Hawk, before you leave the stadium, there's just one thing that's really been bugging me."

"What's that?"

"There's a section of the stadium that wouldn't buckle if the blast pattern fell according to the scenarios I've run."

"And that section is?"

"It's a portion of the luxury boxes. Do you think this is by design?"

Hawk huffed. "When has Al Hasib ever done something that wasn't by design? They try to infuse meaning or purpose into everything they do."

"Do you think they're trying to protect someone?"

Hawk was silent for a few seconds, contemplating about what to tell her. "I think they're trying to kill the G-8 dignitaries."

"What makes you think that?"

"I saw my fa—Thomas Colton—earlier today. And he told me that he was going to be hobnobbing with the G-8 leaders. Taking out all those leaders would be a feather in the cap of Al Hasib. It'd be great recruiting material, not to mention wildly popular the world over for everyone who hates all these G-8 nations."

"And how are they going to kill all those leaders if there isn't a bomb there?" she asked. "Please don't tell me what I think you're about to say."

"They're not planning on striking in a traditional method. No, this has to be up close and personal."

"A suicide bomber?" Alex said with a gasp.

"Bingo. This whole assignment just got that much more interesting, didn't it?"

"And dangerous. Be safe out there, Hawk."

"Aren't I always?"

"Like I said, *be safe.*"

CHAPTER 33

SENATOR MARK ADAMS SETTLED into his seat and checked his watch. He was honored to receive such a prestigious assignment, contrived as it may have been. President Michaels handpicked Adams for a task that every politically-minded person in Washington would cut off their right arm for—but hardly any of them would want it if they knew what it entailed. Entertaining the G-8 leaders around Washington and then at Nationals Park sounded like an enviable job, but Adams knew he was marching the men to their deaths.

He convinced himself it was a necessary evil, the kind of evil that could help restore trust in the American government. But that was only after the American people had lost all hope. Riding into a situation fraught with danger and impending doom, the U.S. government wanted to serve as the cavalry. At least, that's how Adams viewed the situation in his mind. He had to engage in some serious mental gymnastics to arrive at a place where he felt confident he was doing the right thing—and eventually, he did. It wasn't a foreign practice to him, something he learned within the first week of arriving in Washington as a freshman senator. But it was a necessary practice in order to assuage his guilty conscience.

Adams shook the hand of Julien Girard, the prime minister of France, and entered into frivolous banter. Girard, who'd taken the seat next to Adams, surprised him with extensive knowledge of the game of baseball.

"And here I thought you only understood the nuances of soccer," Adams said, forcing a smile before he slapped Girard on the back.

Girard wasn't amused and turned to his left in search of a new conversation partner.

Adams let out an exasperated breath.

"*Stuck up, bastard*," Adams muttered as he stood to leave.

Girard grabbed Adams by the arm and forcefully pulled him down into his seat. "If you think you are being funny, you are mistaken," Girard said. "Don't insult me like that again."

Adams wrestled his arm free from Girard and threw both hands in the air in a gesture of surrender. "I promise, I'll never insult you again—*ever.*"

Or speak to you either.

Free from Girard's fierce grip, Adams walked away, firing one last salvo in the form of a sneering expression.

Adams's mentor tried to convince him that he needed to *kiss ass often* if he hoped to be effective in Washington. "Firmly planted lips in private will earn you pecks in public that will fuel your career," he'd once told Adams.

But after more than two decades of playing Washington's warped game, Adams decided he was done with it. He wanted to actually get something done, and that started with enacting a plan that would help the United States truly secure its borders. Ever since the September 11 bombing, Americans lived in a state of perpetual fear that terrorists would strike again. Yet outside of a few random attempts that never killed more than a dozen or so people at best, the country had never been safer. However, Adams believed a reckoning was coming, at least it was if somebody didn't do something about it. President Michaels was a man who shared Adams's perspective on the future and wanted to take action.

Adams's initially struggled with the unsavory method Michaels proposed. But once Adams convinced himself it was necessary, he embraced it.

Adams checked his watch again. It was time to leave.

CHAPTER 34

WHEN HAWK RETURNED to Nationals Park, he headed straight for the elevators taking him to the luxury suites. Colton put Hawk's name on a guest list, allowing him access to the exclusive and highly secure area.

Inside the private suite, Hawk absorbed the scene. Foreign dignitaries, all clutching glasses in their hands, conversed with various Washington celebrities. A few prominent senators, the quarterback of the Washington Redskins, several world-renowned Wall Street bank CEOs, and a rock star made the suite alive with intriguing conversations. Thomas Colton's presence also livened up the festivities. The smell of freshly carved roast beef emanating from a table in one corner mixed with the powerful aroma of seasoned shrimp at a station in the other corner. For a moment, Hawk was tempted to get something to eat.

He started to look around the room for any signs

of anyone who might be nervous. The first pitch was thrown to the approval of the roaring crowd in the stands. Most the dignitaries barely noticed.

Hawk kept scanning the room before Alex's voice returned in his ear, a voice that was much calmer than earlier.

"What do you see, Hawk?" she asked.

"A bunch of rich dudes eating delicious food," he said. "Should I get a to-go plate for you?"

"Only if it's served with a side of an Al Hasib operative."

"What about a senator trying to make a break for it?"

"And who might that be?"

Hawk's eyes narrowed. "That looks like none other than Senator Mark Adams to me."

Hawk stepped directly in front of Adams's path to the exit. When he came to Hawk, the senator tried to side-step him. But Hawk wasn't having any of it. He slid in front of Adams's path again and again. After Hawk's moves created an uncomfortable two-step of sorts, Adams's resolve intensified. He put his shoulder into Hawk and tried to push his way past.

Hawk put his right hand on Adams's chest.

"Going somewhere?"

Adams glared at him. "I don't know who you think you are, but you need to step aside."

"Not until you answer a few questions for me first."

"Sorry, pal, but I don't have time for your games. Now, if you'll excuse me."

Hawk put his hand on Adams's shoulders, squeezing hard. "Not until you tell me what I need to know."

Adams shook free of Hawk's grip and stepped back. "Do you have a problem? Or do I need to call security over here?"

Hawk narrowed his eyes. "Where are you going in such a hurry? The game just started."

"I have a private matter to attend to—and it's urgent."

Hawk held his ground. "I have an urgent matter as well. And it involves the well-being of the thousands of people in this ballpark."

"Then I suggest you speak with security about it. Now, step aside or I will get security involved."

Hawk moved a half step and put his shoulder into Adams as he walked by. Then Hawk grabbed Adams and pulled him close. "I'm going to hunt you down after this is all over with. I know what you're doing."

Hawk released Adams, who didn't look back as he exited the suite. If Hawk had his way, he would've pummeled some answers out of Adams, but if security hauled him off again, he wouldn't be of much use to the people who were blissfully unaware their lives were in his hands.

Hawk circled the room, searching for a suspicious person or object. In his first cursory glance, nothing seemed unusual.

"Having fun, Son?" Thomas Colton asked as he approached Hawk.

Hawk chose to ignore the annoying suggestion that the man in front of him was his father. They both knew it wasn't true, and the facade still irked Hawk.

"Something bad is going to happen here," Hawk said.

Colton ignored him. "A simple thank you for getting me on the guest list would've sufficed."

"I wouldn't stay here for long. If you see me leave, you might want to leave too."

"Trouble follows you around, doesn't it?"

Hawk took a deep breath and decided to make one more sweep.

CHAPTER 35

MUDIN WAITED IN THE CONCOURSE for the man who was going to slip him a pass for the Silver Slugger Suite. He tried to go through each step mentally. Where he would place the vest to not draw attention yet still inflict maximum damage? How he would do it in a way that no one would notice? Then his mind drifted toward myriad scenarios. What if his rigged detonator didn't go off? Would it trigger a nationwide manhunt for him? A global manhunt? Who would he rather find him first—Al Hasib or the U.S. government? Or would he just take his own life?

With nothing else to pass the time than to wonder about the future, Mudin scanned the concourse anxiously for the man who'd let him end all the speculation. It was only a matter of minutes before Mudin would put his plan into action.

Then he saw the man heading toward him. The tell was that his contact would be wearing a special edition green Washington Nationals cap and eating a plain pretzel. Mudin couldn't miss the man, who was dressed in a suit. It was common to see men dressed in suits for most games at the stadium, but it wasn't the norm for weekend tilts.

The man slid a pass into Mudin's hands without anyone noticing. Mudin tucked it into his pocket and glanced around at the people milling around the concourse. To him, the people appeared as mindless zombies. It was as if such a decadent outing at the park was an obligation instead of a privilege. A couple of kids threw tantrums, begging their fathers to give them ice cream. He watched in shock as a woman wearing a tight-fitting pair of jean shorts didn't flinch when her boyfriend slapped her on the butt and instead of getting upset, she simply reached behind her and held his hand there.

And they all have no idea they'll be dead in about fifteen minutes.

Mudin basked in his moral superiority for a moment, partly because he felt it was real but also because it helped assuage his conflicted conscience.

He strode toward the elevators leading to the private suite on the third level. It was time to follow through with his plan.

Mudin tugged at his vest and reached into his pocket for his second cell phone. He simply wanted to make sure it was there. His phone buzzed with a text message from Fazil. It simply read, "Make Islam proud. Make Al Hasib proud."

Mudin took a deep breath. This was what he intended to do, all while planning his wily escape. He stepped onto an elevator and moved forward with the next part of his plan: disable the live feed.

He snipped the wires, which drew an almost immediate text from Fazil again: "Live feed down. What happened?"

Mudin texted back: "Don't know. Just stepped onto an elevator."

Then Mudin stepped off the elevator. He went directly to the access point and flashed his pass.

Mudin looked around at the men he was about to kill and sighed.

You can do this. You can do this.

Mudin retreated to the restroom where he planned to take his vest off and package it small enough that no one would notice it when he carried it out into the public dining area. But before he could pull his arm out of his sleeve, his phone buzzed, his son's face appearing on the display screen.

"Tabiq," Mudin said. "I'm so glad you called."

"Where are you?" Talib inquired.

"I'm at a baseball game. But don't worry, I still like cricket more."

Mudin blinked hard and tried to resist the urge to cry. He stared at his phone, running his finger across every contour of Talib's face—as if it even really mattered. Talib was going to think his father had died. It was a cruel punishment, but it was necessary if they were going to have a real future.

Mudin told his son he loved him and hung up. He started to pull one of his arms out of the vest when he froze.

I can't do this. I can't kill all these people. I can't leave my son and wife.

Any moral superiority he'd felt only moments before had vanished beneath a tidal wave of guilt. The men and women in the room just beyond the restroom door also likely had sons and daughters, just like he did. They were also someone else's son or daughter. It was a line of thinking he'd been taught to ascribe to at a young age. But Al Hasib tried to make him forget all of that.

"Just do what *feels* right," one of his Al Hasib colleagues once had told him.

Yet it was that lingering idea—the one that encouraged him to do whatever felt right—that caused him to abandon his mission. A difficult dilemma morphed into an impossible situation, one that Mudin suddenly couldn't endorse, even if it was all by his own making.

Mudin exited the restroom. If there was another way, he'd find it. Otherwise, he'd utilize the vest while he was alone, far away from anyone else. He still had time to think, that is until someone brought attention to his Arab appearance.

"Hey, you," a man yelled. "Stop right there."

Mudin didn't want trouble, but he didn't want to be questioned either. Without hesitating, he dashed toward the door.

CHAPTER 36

HAWK'S SECOND AND FINAL SWEEP netted at least one terrified look from a young man, who looked suspicious. For starters, the man was Arabic, easily identifiable from thirty meters across the room. But the man also wasn't interested in sticking around either.

He glanced over his shoulder at Hawk before taking off running.

Hawk followed in pursuit, nearly bowling over a security guard as he went by. Instead, Hawk kept the man upright while discreetly lifting the guard's firearm.

Another security guard attempted to join Hawk in his pursuit of the man.

"If he gets to the main concourse, we're screwed," the guard said with a snarl.

"I'm not gonna let that happen," Hawk said loudly.

After about a minute, they hit the main

concourse—and the mystery man was nowhere to be found.

The security guard, who went by the name Jermaine Cook, radioed to the security with a status update on the man who escaped Hawk's grasp.

"Try to keep up, Cook," Hawk said. "If you can't, I'm going to leave you in the dust."

Cook fell down. "Just go on without me," he said. "I'll find other ways to pass the time."

Hawk preferred it that way. Zipping through the crowds on his own as opposed to babysitting an overweight glorified mall cop? Hawk knew which option he'd choose a hundred out of a hundred times.

Free to pursue the man without any inhibitions, Hawk took off. He thought he saw a glimpse of the man's hat, though he wondered if the terrorist had thrown it away at some point. Then he caught a whir out of the corner of his eye near the turnstiles.

Hawk followed suit, ripping through the admission gate and chasing the man down the stairs toward the street.

"Alex," Hawk began, "where are you at? Are you with me?"

"Oh, I'm here," she said. "What do you need help with?"

"Can you put a satellite on my position? I want to see if you can spot the terrorist and tell me where he's going next."

"I'll do my best, Hawk."

Hawk heard plenty of clicking on the keyboard, which gave him hope that she'd yield results. After a few long seconds, she returned with an efficient way.

"Got an answer for me?"

"Go to Dock 79. It looks like that's where he's headed."

Dock 79 was a waterfront apartment complex built on the banks of the Anacostia River, just across the street from Nationals Park. And it was the perfect place to disappear.

"Tap into the security feed there," Hawk said. "I need to know where he's headed."

"Roger that," Alex replied.

Hawk danced through the slow-moving traffic on the road right outside Nationals Park, mouthing apologies to the drivers who laid on their horns. Once he reached the other side, he sprinted toward the main entrance of Dock 79.

"Talk to me, Alex," he said.

"He took the stairwell and went up."

"All the way?"

"That's what it looked like, but I still haven't seen him emerge on the roof."

Hawk rushed onto an empty elevator once he slipped into the lobby and selected the highest floor.

Once he got out, he sought to go even higher by locating the stairwell and ascending to the roof. He pulled out the gun he'd lifted off the guard and crept outside.

Hawk crouched low as he wove in and out of a maze of air conditioning units.

"You've got nowhere to hide now," Hawk said. "Come out with your hands in the air."

"Stay away," a man said.

Hawk spun in the direction of the water and saw a man standing on the ledge with his hands in the air. Hawk trained his gun on the man, continuing to walk toward him.

"I'm warning you—stay back," the man said.

"We need to talk," Hawk said. "I found four explosive devices in the stadium. I'm assuming that you planted them there. Are there any more?"

The man's phone rang.

"I need to answer this or someone may detonate my vest remotely," he said. "I don't think you'd want that."

Hawk gestured for the man to go ahead, but Hawk refused to drop his weapon.

Slowly, the man reached into his pocket and pulled out a phone. "I'm a little busy right now," he said. He waited for a moment. "I don't know what's wrong with the video transmitter, but I'm in the restroom. I'll be there in a minute." Another pause. "Perhaps something went wrong with the detonators, but at least I'll be able to finish the most important part of the job."

The man hung up.

"Having seconds thoughts?" Hawk asked.

The man slid his phone into his pocket and nodded. "I don't want to hurt anyone."

"Neither do I," Hawk said. "Why don't you step down from that ledge, remove your vest, and let's talk about it?"

"There were only four devices, but you need to step back."

Hawk continued to walk toward the man, who glanced over his shoulder at the river behind him nine stories below.

"That's a long fall. I'm not sure you want to do that," Hawk said, continuing his steady gait.

"I said *stay away*."

"It's clear that you've had a change of heart and you don't want to hurt anyone," Hawk said. "Neither do I." He dropped his gun. "Let's just talk for a minute."

"You don't understand. Someone else could detonate this vest at any moment."

Hawk stopped and cocked his head to one side. "Sounds like someone doesn't trust you. Sounds like someone turned you into a weapon without giving you a choice."

"I have a choice, and I'm about to make it."

"And what kind of choice is that?"

"I'm going to blow up this vest so that no one gets hurt."

Hawk walked closer and had edged within ten feet of the man. "You don't have to die like this," Hawk said. "In fact, you don't have to die at all."

"You don't understand. They'll kill my entire family if I'm still alive."

"Then let's trick them. Take the vest off and throw it in the water."

"I can't," the man said. "It measures my biometrics. If I take it off, they'll know and set it off. I only have one option."

The man leaned back and started to fall. Hawk rushed toward the man and grabbed his leg before he vanished over the side. Hawk held tightly to the man's leg as he dangled over the roof.

"Just take off the vest now."

"No, they'll detonate it immediately. And it'll kill us both. You have to let me go. If I go into the water, it'll short circuit the vest and I can take it off."

Hawk glanced at the water. "You may not survive the fall."

"It's my only option at this point."

"Are you sure?"

"Just let go," the man said.

"You haven't even told me your name," Hawk said.

"Malik. Malik Mudin."

"Good luck, Malik," Hawk said before releasing the man.

Mudin began his rapid descent toward the water.

CHAPTER 37

MUDIN FELT THE WIND rush against his face as he started falling. He was certain that the world was in desperate need of change, but he was also certain that Al Hasib's way wasn't it. And it took him strapping on a suicide vest and contemplating his own humanity—and mortality—to realize it.

Mudin was amazed at how many thoughts he could have in such a short period of time, how he could consider so many things in a matter of fleeting seconds. He didn't know if he'd survive or not, yet he had plenty of regrets. He wished he'd been a better husband to his wife, as well as a better father to Tabiq. If something went awry, they'd both grow up without a spouse and a dad, respectively. A widow and a fatherless child—their fate in their culture would be a cruel one unless someone saw it fit to redeem their situation. And all of that seemed suspect, even if he survived.

Mudin could see the water getting closer and closer. He had no idea if the murky waters below were five meters deep or fifty. And it mattered. One he could survive, the other might not.

He closed his eyes and prayed to Allah, asking for favor and safety.

In an instant, nothing no longer mattered for Mudin.

His vest exploded a few feet before impact, rocking the apartment complex above him.

CHAPTER 38

HAWK WITHDREW FROM THE LEDGE the moment he recognized the explosion. The building shook, and he dove to the ground to avoid any shrapnel. He couldn't believe Malik Mudin was dead. Hawk bit his lip and shook his head. He rarely had the opportunity to save someone, and this time he'd failed in his bid to do so. Mudin's body was strewn across the Anacostia River. He'd likely never be identified, but Hawk would know along with the people who made the decision to pull the trigger.

"Did you see that?" Hawk asked into his com link.

"I saw it all," Alex said. "What a shame. Seemed like he wanted to do the right thing."

"I agree, but we'll never know now."

"Well, the mission wasn't a bust. We did save the lives of thousands of people and prevented President Michaels's administration from gaining an opportunity to railroad the American people with a bogus claim about lack of security."

"Yes, we do have something to celebrate," Hawk said. "But we also missed our chance to find out where Fazil might have been hiding."

"We're gonna catch him, you know. He won't be able to run forever."

"And when we do …" Hawk trailed off, leaving the rest of his thought unsaid. But he knew that Alex would know how to complete it.

"I do have some good news though," she said.

"What's that?"

"Check your phone. I just sent you some footage that you might want to see."

Hawk pulled out his phone and watched a security video feed of Senator Adams interacting with Malik Mudin. One of the clips was from several weeks prior, while the other was from earlier that afternoon.

"I hope you have high resolution footage of this," he said.

"I do—and I already sent it to the FBI."

"Excellent. When do you think we'll see him arrested?"

"It won't take long with that kind of evidence. I also included a line in my email about the location of the C-4 explosive devices and where they could be found. I wanted to make sure they traced all of the supplies back to Adams."

"And you think they'll be able to?"

"I also hacked his personal credit card account and found charges from corresponding companies that produce those same materials used to make those explosive devices."

"Did you include those in the file?"

Alex laughed. "Oh, Hawk, when are you going to realize I'm not an amateur?"

He smiled. "That's what I like to hear."

"So is a celebration in order tonight?" she asked.

"I was thinking about a Bollywood marathon. What do you say?"

"That might be just what the doctor ordered."

CHAPTER 39

HAWK AWOKE THE NEXT MORNING to the ringing of his phone. He moaned as he rolled over on the couch to see who was calling. There was only one person he'd answer for, aside from Alex, who was sound asleep in his bed. He never considered for a moment to send her home late at night by herself— or let her sleep on the couch. And he wasn't ready to do anything that would compromise their working chemistry. Not yet, anyway.

Hawk glanced at the screen on his phone. It was Blunt.

"Good work, Hawk," Blunt said. "I saw what you did yesterday."

"It was in the news already?"

"Don't worry. Nobody has identified you publicly yet, so your cover is probably safe for now. But it'll be impossible to remain incognito forever. This is the age of social media, and any idiot with a phone can essentially turn into a television reporter from yesteryear."

"That's what I'm afraid of."

"Well, don't let it stop you from doing a damn fine job like you did with this latest threat."

"If you hadn't heard about it …"

"We can't dwell on the what-ifs in life, good or bad. What happened, happened. Now we must move forward, casting a suspicious eye everywhere. But that's the nature of what we do, Hawk. We can't trust anyone. And I mean *anyone*."

Hawk rolled over on the couch. "So, I doubt you called this morning just to tell me that."

"No, unfortunately, I didn't. I need you and Alex to get to Morocco as soon as possible."

"Is something wrong?"

"Yes, but it's not something I can talk about on the phone. I've got another assignment for you. And this time, the stakes are just as high as they've ever been."

"Morocco, huh?"

"Tangier to be exact. I've already booked you a pair of tickets since my pilot is on another assignment. You can pick up your boarding passes at the gate."

"What time does this flight leave?"

"Three hours from now, so you need to hurry."

Hawk hung up and sighed. He sat upright and rubbed his face with his hands.

Am I dreaming? Couldn't Blunt have given us a couple of days off?

As a former Navy Seal, Hawk knew that terrorists didn't take time off in their scheming and plotting. And terrorists all recognized that the best way to unleash an attack was right after the U.S. was reeling from another one. Citizens might be more diligent, but the government was going to be stuck in a seemingly eternal cycle of answering questions and looking for answers as to how to prevent it from ever happening again. Hawk took a deep breath and stood up. His hard work was just beginning—and if Blunt needed him in Tangier, then that's where they'd go.

Hawk knocked on the door to his room, waking up Alex.

"Got to get moving," he said. "Blunt booked us tickets for a flight to Tangier in less than three hours from now."

"Okay, okay," she said. "I'm getting up and getting ready."

Hawk smiled, happy that his getting ready consisted of throwing a few clothes into a bag and putting a hat on.

As he was walking out the door, his phone rang again. This time, it was Thomas Colton.

"Brady, it's your fa—it's Thomas Colton. I wanted to congratulate you on a job well done yesterday."

"Thanks. Just doing my job," Hawk said.

"Well, you went above and beyond. I'm glad you're okay and nobody was hurt."

"Actually, somebody was hurt yesterday."

"Who? That terrorist scum?"

"He wasn't exactly a willing participant," Hawk said. "He wanted to walk out, but Al Hasib makes sure their operatives don't get cold feet. You would've thought his recruits understood that by now."

"They're weaponizing people?"

"It's more or less what they've been doing for years—except now if you protest, they detonate for you."

"Sick bastards," Colton said.

"That's why I do what I do," Hawk quipped.

"And that's why I do what I do, too."

Hawk bit his tongue. He appreciated using Colton Industries' state-of-the-art technology, but he hated when it fell in the hands of evil people. After seeing all the destruction wreaked all over the globe, Hawk wasn't convinced that one side ever truly held the moral high ground in a conflict.

"We do what we can, right?" said Hawk, who couldn't have kept a straight face if he said that in Colton's presence. But over the phone, he got away with it sounding genuine.

"Good luck, Son—I mean, Brady," Colton said. "This is hard for me."

"I know, Mr. Colton. I know."

***

AT DULLES INTERNATIONAL AIRPORT, Hawk sauntered up to the counter with Alex to claim their tickets. The lady who assisted him was surprisingly helpful and pressed his tickets into his hand once he showed her their fake passports. He turned to look at Alex.

"Have a nice flight, Mr. Young," the customer service representative said.

He smiled at her and then turned to Alex.

"You ready?" he asked.

Alex nodded.

"Morocco, here we come."

Hawk stopped by one of the bars and ducked inside when he saw a cable news program showing a video of President Michaels.

"Check this out," Hawk said to Alex.

They both stood and watched Michaels deliver his speech. The title above the scrolling updates recapping the highlights of his address to the American people was a title that made Hawk sick: President Michaels Discusses Terrorism Threats.

"Yesterday, one our secret operatives thwarted an attack on Nationals Park," Michaels said. "As leading dignitaries from G-8 nations converged upon Washington, terrorists attempted to inflict more pain and suffering on the American people for no reason. Next week, I will be giving Congress a bill that I believe will help tighten our borders and keep our country even safer from attacks like these from even being conceived on our soil."

Alex turned to Hawk. "Seen enough yet?"

Hawk shook his head and sighed. "Welcome to the United Nanny State of America."

"Michaels needs to be *stopped*," she whispered.

"In due time, Alex. In due time."

As they hustled along toward the terminal, Hawk's phone buzzed with a text message. He looked at the screen and read the message.

He told Alex to go ahead without him.

"Are you crazy, Hawk?" she asked.

Hawk cleared his throat hard, hoping that she got the hint that she wasn't to refer to him by his real name in such a public setting.

"I'm sorry, *Mr. Young*?" she corrected herself.

"To answer your question, yes, I am crazy," he said. "But I will make it there before the cabin door shuts, okay?"

She shrugged. "Whatever."

"When nature calls …"

She kept walking, refusing to acknowledge his

last comment with nothing more than a flippant hand wave.

Hawk looked down at his screen again and reread the message:

. **"We need to talk. Go into the next family restroom on your right. – ET"**

Hawk knew it was her—Emily Thornton. That was the signature way she signed all her text messages. If she wanted him to call her, she would simply text him with the message "ET". Hawk laughed, understanding the code as "phone home". No one else could know that about them. It had to be her, though if he was honest with himself, it wasn't the wisest decision he'd ever made. Someone else could ambush him in there and leave him for dead.

But he was too curious. Alex was convinced she saw Emily at the Searchlight headquarters a few days earlier. There were too many unlikely events happening so close together for Hawk to simply chalk it up as coincidence. It had to be Emily.

Hawk checked his surroundings before twisting the door handle and tugging on it to gain entry. He hurried inside and prepared for an assault—but there was no need.

Emily Thornton was standing against the back wall.

A flood of emotions washed over Hawk. He'd been processing the fact that she might actually be alive for a while since Alex first shared her hunch with him. But when he actually saw Emily, he didn't know whether to kiss her or punch her lights out.

"Emily, I-I." He paused. "I don't know what to say."

"Shut up and let me do the talking," she said. "I don't have much time, so I need to make this quick. But there's something you need to know."

CHAPTER 40

HAWK HUSTLED ONTO THE PLANE, dragging his luggage behind. He stuffed his bag into the over-head bin, cramming his jacket next to it. A lady across the aisle watched closely as he played Tetris with the luggage to make everything fit so the door would close.

"Don't you wish the airlines and luggage makers would get together on the size of bins and carry-on bags?" he said to her.

She forced a smile and returned to reading her book.

Hawk settled into his seat and latched the belt across his lap.

"I was beginning to wonder if you were going to make it," Alex said, flipping the pages of the inflight magazine without looking up.

"There are some things you can't rush," he said.

"Who texted you?"

"An old friend."

"Do I know this old friend?"

Hawk shook his head. "I don't think so. Just an old colleague of mine. It was no big deal."

Alex shoved the magazine back into the seat pocket in front of her and looked at Hawk.

"So, how do you propose we pass the time on this flight since we can't really talk about work in public?"

Hawk smiled. "If only we had a Bollywood movie to watch." He reached down and pulled out his briefcase, which contained a laptop and several DVDs.

A grin broke across Alex's face. "If only," she said, grabbing the DVDs to inspect the small collection.

Hawk slipped his ear buds in as Alex took hold of the laptop and set up the movie. He leaned back and closed his eyes, more confused than he'd ever been. He didn't know what to make of his conversation with Emily. It could change everything. But he tried not to think about it. He just wanted to go to sleep and revel in the victories he'd accomplished over the past week, though it didn't necessarily feel that way.

Hawk and Alex kept the Jordanian Prime Minister from orphaning his daughter, while Hawk watched a man die for his son in a roundabout way. The man exploded right before he made impact with the water.

A second or two later, and the bomb never would've detonated. But there was a stadium full of people who didn't die at the hands of Al Hasib, a fact that should've put Hawk in a celebratory mood.

But he didn't feel like doing anything. He wasn't sure what was going on—or what was right side up in his topsy-turvy world. He'd even started to lose faith in the very government he believed in, or at least he lost faith in the people running the government.

Hawk had to do the only thing he knew how. He had to keep fighting.

THE END

ACKNOWLEDGMENTS

I am grateful to so many people who have helped with the creation of this project and the entire Brady Hawk series. Morocco is one of my favorite places I've ever visited and loved setting some scenes in the book there.

Krystal Wade has been a fantastic help in handling the editing of this book, and Dwight Kuhlman has produced another great audio version for your listening pleasure.

I would also like to thank my advance reader team for all their input in improving this book along with all the other readers who have enthusiastically embraced the story of Brady Hawk. Stay tuned ... there's more Brady Hawk coming soon.

ABOUT THE AUTHOR

R.J. PATTERSON is an award-winning writer living in southeastern Idaho. He first began his illustrious writing career as a sports journalist, recording his exploits on the soccer fields in England as a young boy. Then when his father told him that people would pay him to watch sports if he would write about what he saw, he went all in. He landed his first writing job at age 15 as a sports writer for a daily newspaper in Orangeburg, S.C. He later attended earned a degree in newspaper journalism from the University of Georgia, where he took a job covering high school sports for the award-winning *Athens Banner-Herald* and *Daily News*.

He later became the sports editor of *The Valdosta Daily Times* before working in the magazine world as an editor and freelance journalist. He has won numerous writing awards, including a national award for his investigative reporting on a sordid tale surrounding an NCAA investigation over the University of Georgia football program.

R.J. enjoys the great outdoors of the Northwest while living there with his wife and three children. He still follows sports closely. He also loves connecting with readers and would love to hear from you. To stay updated about future projects, connect with him over Facebook or on the interwebs at www.RJPbooks.com and sign up for his newsletter to get deals and updates.

Made in the USA
Middletown, DE
26 October 2018